W9-AOM-888

THE
SWEET
SUMMER

THE SWEET SUMMER

A NOVEL

WILLIAM KELLEY

Westminster John Knox Press
Louisville, Kentucky

Book design by Sharon Adams

First edition
Published by Westminster John Knox Press
Louisville, Kentucky

This book is printed on acid-free paper that meets the American National Standards Institute Z39.48 standard. ♾

PRINTED IN THE UNITED STATES OF AMERICA
00 01 02 03 04 05 06 07 08 09 — 10 9 8 7 6 5 4 3 2 1

Library of Congress Cataloging-in-Publication Data

Kelley, William, 1929–
The sweet summer / William Kelley.
p. cm.
ISBN 0-664-22224-2
1. Male friendship—Southern States—Fiction. 2. Southern States—Race relations—Fiction. 3. United States. Air Force—Fiction. 4. Afro-American boxers—Fiction. I. Title.

PS3561.E39 S94 2000
813′.54—dc21

99–05928

While I certainly hope that there will
be some similarity between
my characters and real people,
it is necessary for me to state
that any painful correspondences
between them and actual persons
living or dead are purely
matters of coincidence.

For Nina

. . . the Sweet Science of Bruising.

Pierce Egan,
English Boxing Historian

Quoted in "The Sweet Science:
Boxing and Boxiana—A Ringside View."
A. J. Liebling, *The New Yorker,* 1950

I don't want to knock my opponent out.
I want to hit him,
step away,
and watch him hurt.
I want his heart.

Joe Frazier

I try to catch my opponent on the tip of his nose
because I try to punch the bone into his brain.

Mike Tyson

Down there in the stable
a hollow square of faces
in the lantern light,
the white faces on three sides,
the black faces on the fourth,
and in the center
two of [Sutpen's] wild negroes fighting,
naked,
fighting not as white men fight,
with rules and weapons,
but as negroes fight,
to hurt one another
quick and bad.

William Faulkner, *Absalom, Absalom!*

You eased up on that boy! Don't you be goin' white on me.

Wash Washington

THE TEAM

Master Sergeant C. George "Wash" Washington, former professional heavyweight, with a voice like an asphalt tuba and a heart as big as Avery Island, where he came from. Wash knew every promoter and manager in the boxing South. He would have given his life in a minute for any one of his "boys."

Staff Sergeant Ezekiel "Ace" Kingdom, our corner/cut man, who looked like he had just helped Lazarus out of his tomb. A master with the styptic, the cold iron, and the smelling salts. He loved boxing like no man I've ever known.

Laverne "Chappie" Chapman, heavyweight. A sweet-natured fisherman from Mooringsport, Louisiana. Chappie could play the twelve-string guitar country-style and was always composing songs about our journey, including "How Madden Got Us Busted." He loved Huddie Ledbetter, and near the end he could do a damned good imitation.

Caldwell "Coop" Cooper, light-heavyweight. An Adonis. A New Orleans boy with an insatiable appetite for women. Coop and I roomed together, and he would bring his ladies up to the room when we had twin beds. A real education. A master boxer, who became my best friend.

Cully Madden, middleweight. Your obedient narrator.

Thutmose "Mose" Oates, junior middleweight. Pure country, from Ninety-Six, South Carolina. A quiet, lovesick, gentle man who wrote every day to his girlfriend back home. His father was doing life for murder at the Louisiana State Farm at Angola.

Wilson "Waldo" Waldron, welterweight. A joker, cutup, with the fastest hands I have ever seen. He came from a coal town in West Virginia and always called me "boss." He did not like fighting white boys because they were "unconscionably foul."

THE TEAM

Dwayne "Sonny" Bliss, lightweight. May have been an idiot savant. He could glance at a number of almost anything and tell you exactly how many there were. He'd glance at a menu and then recite it, including prices. He saved us a lot of money finding errors in restaurant checks and hotel bills. He made nothing of his uncanny abilities. A fine boxer, a warrior's soul.

Bobby Ray "Stone" Livingstone, featherweight. A very private man who always looked guilty whether he was or he wasn't. He loved mirrors. Chappie said, "He got to have a mirror so that he know he *there*!" A somehow wounded person, not very likeable, but the balls of a lion.

Tremaine "Spider" Webb, bantamweight. A courtly, dapper, charming man who spoke English and Creole French with a casual precision. His interest in the black arts and voodoo was extraordinary and very informed. He loved graveyards, and I think he was some kind of necromantic adept. He always wanted to read my tarot, but I wouldn't let him.

ONE

I got stones in my passway
and my road seem dark as night.

Robert Johnson, "Stones In My Passway"

It is now clear to me that I wouldn't have gotten anywhere near a boxing team if it hadn't been for Mr. James Joyce. Him and his wretched *Ulysses*. I was all set to go, and my mother was outside in the car honking the horn and yelling that I had better get my ass down there in thirty seconds or I could by God walk to Albany. So I zipped up my ditty bag and started out of the bedroom quickstep but suddenly thought of something to read, and James Joyce practically leaped off the shelf into my left hand.

Mom was doing about fifty up the dirt road toward the county highway when she noticed the book, and let out a screech about filthy Irish bastards, and she was doing about eighty by the time she hit the intersection and turned right, proceeded through a three-sixty, sheared off old man Hoyer's mailbox, and roared off north shouting that James Joyce was a drunken degenerate who wrote about nothing but sex-crazed sluts diddling themselves on rusty pisspots.

By the time we got to the armory in Albany, she had progressed from pisspots to sodomy, assuring me that the Army was full of practicing perverts and that I should by God watch my back. She was ordering me always to take showers alone when she was more or less interrupted by sideswiping a taxicab. Our goodbyes were cut short as she alighted on the diminutive cab driver, swinging her purse and assuring him that he was obviously a Mafia bagman and if she had only remembered to bring her pistol she would march him down to the nearest police station and have him booked for misprision of felony. The poor cabby was trying to take refuge behind a passing bus the last I saw of him.

I had gotten through my physical and was sitting in my drawers in a bare room with ten other candidates when Mr. Joyce's book first became an issue. The others were making small talk about the oath we were waiting to take when the big kid next to me turned and said:

"The hell you reading?"

"An Irish novel." I showed him the cover.

"Useless?"

"That's close enough."

"Hey! This guy's reading a book name of useless!"

There wasn't much reaction, even though the big kid—whose name was Dickess—repeated himself and tried to drum up some laughter. He didn't, but the battle had been joined—and so had James Joyce and I, hip and thigh, with Dickess on the bagpipes. Why it took me almost three months to knock Dickess on his ass, I don't know, but it certainly had nothing to do with my mother's salutary example.

TWO

I got to keep movin' . . .
Blues fallin' down like hail
And the days keeps on worryin' me
there's a hellhound on my trail.

Robert Johnson, "Hell Hound On My Trail"

Sometime in the middle of that spring, I began to have a recurrent dream that I had enlisted in the Army, had been sent to Texas for eight weeks of forced march and emaciation, getting needles stuck in my arms, legs, and the orifice of my fundament; then getting shipped off to study codes and ciphers in an Illinois swamp. A terrible dream, always culminating in something truly monstrous—such as cleaning a latrine whose commodes kept violently reverse-flushing, sending great brown gouts of their deposits ceilingward and then plopping down at me while I ran about waving a wire toilet brush in futile attempts at self-defense. I would wake up in a dithering sweat only to look about, see my fellow inmates snoring and tossing in their bunks, and realize that the awful business was no dream at all.

The Army was in fact the Army Air Corps, the eight weeks had been spent at Lackland Field in Texas, the swamp was Scott Field in Illinois, and the codes and ciphers were the obsessive business of the instructors at the cryptographic school. I didn't want to be a cryptographer, thought of Scott Field as an internment camp with airplanes, and honestly believed that thirty-one more months of army life would unavoidably result in my suffering a cataleptic psychic collapse, or a total passage of the innards, whichever came first.

So that when the proximately causal incident began to occur, I recognized it at once, and welcomed it, thinking that it had a certain inevitability, size, and beauty about it, and that its consequences were in no way going to be minor.

I was sitting on the springs of my bunk with my mattress rolled up behind me, reading the Molly Bloom soliloquy (for about the fifteenth time). It was a Saturday morning, late, with some last few of the troops cleaning themselves up for a weekend pass in St. Louis. The floor of the upper bay was gleaming from last night's assiduous waxing, and I was feeling at peace and almost monastic as I sat there in my nearly solitary splendor. And then it came, rudely and loud, the voice of Private Estes Fox, the Paul Bunyan of the teletype operators.

"Madden! Cully Madden! The hell you at, boy?"

I'd heard the voice before, out on the grinder, when his corporal had let him call cadence for his platoon. Big, Southern, country, full of drawling menace. I put the book over my face and said: "Dear God, it's Holy Saturday. Are you going to let the son-of-a-bitch profane your solemn day?"

"Madden! You Yankee bastard! Always beatin' up on folks! Come on down hyar while I whup your sorry ass!"

A kid named Morton came running down the middle of the bay, a wet towel wrapped around him. "Cully, Cully! Do you hear him?"

"I hear him."

"It's Fox, from over in the second area!"

"Thank you, Mort. It could be no other."

-5-

"Jesus, Cully," Morton said, now at the window looking down. "He's big as a goddamn house."

"I know."

"And he's got his barracks with him!"

"Got it under his arm, does he, Mort?"

"No." Morton looked around at me. "You know what I mean. Must be two dozen of them."

"Madden! You comin' out, or do I have to come get you?"

"Cully, you got to go."

"No, I don't."

Dickess rose on one elbow from where he was napping at the far end of the bay. "What'd you say?"

"Cully, you got to. For the honor of the barracks." Morton looked distraught, as if his world had suddenly tilted. "Cully, you wouldn't back down."

"For the honor of the barracks, Madden."

I closed the book and got to my feet. "Dickess, you wouldn't know honor from a lipfart."

Dickess put his head back down on his pillow and said, "Hot damn. Cully Madden turning chicken."

I went to my footlocker and got out some sneakers and the eight-ounce boxing gloves that I'd bought in San Antonio. The theory was that, if you used gloves, it wasn't a fistfight. It was a boxing match, and, therefore semi-allowable. The theory had no clothes and few defenders. But I always took the gloves along, when I could, as an earnest of civilized conduct.

"You think you can take him, Cully?"

"We're sure going to find out, Mort." And then, as I turned to go: "You better put some pants on if you're going to be my witness."

"Yes, sir! Yes, sir!" Mort shouted, as he ran for his locker. "You're my hero!"

And I walked down toward the stairs thinking that being a hero was mostly a howling pain in the ass.

Fox was a big kid all right, about six-three and two-twenty, with a shaved head that rounded on his square jaw like the dome of a ball peen hammer. He was wearing shorts, and his legs looked like a pair of hairy pilings. I sat down on the porch, pulled on my sneakers, and started lacing them up.

"Hey, you," Fox said.

I ignored him.

"Madden, you deef?"

"Fox, you want it with or without gloves?"

"I don't want no damn gloves."

I nodded, started to get to my feet, and he rushed me, wrapped his arms around me and started a bear hug. I should've figured him for this, but I wasn't at full speed yet. I could feel the wind leaving my lungs. But he was standing straddle-legged, and I managed to turn just enough to lift my right knee smartly into his balls. He issued an astonished grunt, loosened his grip, stared at me pop-eyed, then reared his fat head back preparatory to delivering what would probably have been a very damaging head-butt. But I got my right hand out of bondage just enough to make a fist and plant it on the point of his chin as he brought it forward. He staggered backward, let out an anguished roar, grabbed his balls with one hand, his chin with the other, and, screaming obscenities, charged again.

I met him with three left jabs. I was down off the porch now, on solid ground, and the jabs made the blood start spurting. He hesitated, came on again roaring. I stepped aside and hit him a right in the near ear as he went by. He staggered to one side, skipped into a tight spin, tripped on the concrete frame of the barrack's flat cellar doors, and fell assbackwards and cruciform full upon them. The doors shuddered, splintered at the hinges, and collapsed. Poor Fox, apparently poleaxed, disappeared into the depths without a human sound.

There was a moment of silence among the spectators. Then, "Oh, shit," said Morton. "I think you killed him."

And I was peering dubiously into the hole when there came a lovely, anguished shout: "Goddamn! Somebody help me! My ass is full of splinters!"

Lieutenant Colonel Ball was not notable for his sense of humor. He scowled up at me, a sheaf of papers in his hands.

"You wish to make a statement, Airman?"

"I'm certainly sorry, sir."

"Well, apparently, Airman Fox is a damned sight sorrier." He rattled the papers. "Damage to government property. The two cellar doors, twenty-eight dollars and forty-two cents. Damage to Airman Fox—broken jaw, multiple contusions, multiple splinters—one hundred eighty-six dollars. So far." He looked back up at me sharply. "Are you trying to get yourself an incorrigible discharge?"

"No, sir."

He picked up another paper. "This report from Lieutenant Dye says that, including basic training, you've been involved in fourteen fistfights with your fellow airmen. How do you explain that? How come you're not already in the stockade?"

"Fox was the first one to press charges, sir."

"You intimidated the others?"

"No, sir. They started all the fights."

"Over what?"

"Well, sir, it sort of mushroomed. But in the beginning it was because I like to read books."

"Read books? What the hell did you do? Read them aloud at night?"

I heaved a sigh, and tried to explain about James Joyce, and how it had gotten rapidly out of hand, and how the more I won the fights, the more I was challenged and harassed until it was just one goddamned calamity after another. And I could see no end to it.

The colonel looked at me throughout, nodding slowly, his expression almost disconsolate, as if he realized that the only way to prevent me from going on to all manner of outrages and abominations was to have me summarily shot. When I finished, he looked away, put his hands together, and spoke softly.

"Airman Madden? Have you ever done any boxing?"

THREE

I can tell the wind is risin'
the leaves tremblin' on the tree.

Robert Johnson, "Hell Hound On My Trail"

An hour later I was prowling the Fourth Area (the black enclave) looking for the base gym. The colonel had proposed a way in which I could avoid court-martial. Try out for the boxing team and by God *make* the boxing team, and I wouldn't even have to worry about the statement of charges. He, personally, as athletic officer, would take care of them. I could scarcely believe my ears, but he explained that we were about to leave the Army behind and become the U.S. Air Force and would therefore need our own proper and competitive athletic teams. From what the colonel understood, not a single white man had yet made the team, and he sure as hell did not intend to preside over an all-black team representing the Air Force. No offense to the blacks, of course—just a matter of proper military proportion. I said I'd do my best, and he said my best had damned well better be good enough, or I'd find myself on permanent duty as the chief latrine orderly over in the stockade. The word "latrine" sealed it. I saluted him smartly and assured him I would prevail. He stood up and returned my salute and, at that moment, looked so much like my mother that I almost called him Mom.

The base gym turned out to be the biggest and most neglected building in the Fourth Area. The barracks were bad enough, with their rusted screens and peeling white paint. But the gym was a Quonset disaster, looking rather like some forlorn giant beetle plopped misshapen and untimely out of the eye of an itinerant tornado. It did not look safe to enter. I hesitated for a moment, watching to see if any of the other passersby (not a white face among them) would risk it. None did. So, with genuine trepidation, I took the plunge.

It was worse inside. The floor was buckled and warped. The lines of the big basketball court went wobbling and fading off into foul territory. The huge windows thrust into the rounded sides were crack-paned and sprung, requiring stout chunks of two-by-six to hold them precariously open. And ventilation was definitely needed. Seven boxing rings—three down each side and one larger one in the middle—were all in use, and all around them were other aspirants jumping rope, shadowboxing, or working the heavy and light bags. Sweat gleamed on every body, and that peculiarly pungent aroma of the boxing ring—which I've always thought was half perspiration and half fear—permeated the place. I myself began to sweat immediately.

There was a large man in one corner of the big ring—a master sergeant, his uniform tailored and sharply pressed—who appeared to be in charge of things, so I eased my way out toward the center, trying to circle a rope-muscled young man who was vigorously shadowboxing his way through the crowd. As I tried to pass, he threw a right uppercut that damned near took my nose off.

"Hey, goddamn it!" I shouted.

-11-

"Fuck you, whitey!"

And he was gone in the crowd.

"Hey you!" came a shout from behind me.

I turned. It was the hulking master sergeant with a megaphone.

"You mean me, Sergeant?"

"You. Get your spiny ass over here!"

"Yes, sir." Grins and chuckles all around as I pushed through toward the ring. As I got to the apron, the sergeant was glowering down at me.

"You McFadden?"

"No, sir. Madden. Cully Madden."

"The colonel called me. Said you needed somethin' to hit."

"Well, I wouldn't put it quite that way."

"I don't give a diddley how you put it. You got any kit?"

"I'm wearing it. Under this."

"Must be hot in there. You got a cup on?"

"Yeah."

"Yes, Sergeant. And a mouthpiece?"

"Yes, Sergeant." I took my ancient mouthpiece out of my shirt pocket, stuck one end of it in my mouth.

"Well, all right then," he said. "Man come prepared." He turned, then put the bullhorn to his mouth. "Hey, Cooper!" he shouted. "Coop! Get on over here!" He turned back to me. "Come on up here, boy. I got you somethin' to hit. For damned sure."

I climbed up on the apron. "We using this ring?"

"That's right. Get them fatigues off." He turned to the heavyweights who had been working the ring. "That's it, Chappie. Take that Samoan down to ring four, see if he got any gut."

I was folding my fatigues and laying them on the apron when I saw my opponent arrive. Goddamned black Adonis, I thought. Café au lait, and a hundred-eighty on the hoof. God help the Irish. The sergeant said, "Cooper? This here's the great white hope. So's we don't end up with an all-black team. See if you can't put him down firm but no bad damage."

"What, what?" Cooper said, softly. "He look like a middleweight. We *need* a middleweight."

"Never mind that. See what he made of. But go easy."

Cooper nodded, put his mouthpiece in, turned to address me. He looked unhappy, but resigned to his work.

I climbed into the ring, crossed to the corner where the sergeant was indicating the stool. As I sat down, he asked, "What you weigh?"

"One fifty-eight."

He raised his eyebrows. "You look a little heavier."

"I fight a little heavier," I said, beginning to get annoyed with his condescension.

"Well, I told him to go easy, so you should be all right."

I looked at him. "I never said I'd go easy, and I don't mean to."

He rolled his eyes upward. "Okay, man. It's your jaw."

"He's got his hands wrapped," I said.

"Well, I'll wrap *your* hands," he said, "If you promise not to bite me."

"I don't mean to be difficult," I said. I stuck out my hands and he wrapped them swiftly and expertly, glancing up at me now and then to see if I approved. I nodded as he finished. "Good job."

"Goddamn, I'm relieved," he said, with only slight sarcasm. "Now the gloves."

"Fourteen ounce?" I said.

"That's right. You been a few?"

"A few."

"You got no face marks."

"Lucky."

"Stay lucky. This is a very good boy, hits like billy-be-Jesus."

He turned, sorted in a pile of headgear, found a dry one, clapped it on my head, fastened the chin strap.

"Tighter," I said. He tightened it. "And I'd like some of that Vaseline under my left eye."

"Yes, sir!" he said, eyeing me. He applied the Vaseline, then took the mouthpiece out of my mouth, dipped it in the water bucket, then put it gently back. Then, softly: "You'd best be good, boy. With your high and mighty. Because if you ain't, I'm gonna kick your white ass."

I looked at him with something like a smile. "Yes, sir."

He turned then, looking amused, and spoke to a staff sergeant who had just arrived at ringside, along with a fairly sizable crowd of the curious. "Sergeant Kingdom," he said. "We will have three two-minute rounds. If it goes that long."

"Sergeant Washington," Kingdom said. He put a gold watch down on the apron, picked up a small hammer, addressed a small, wood-mounted bell. "Upon your signal, Sergeant."

Washington walked to the center of the ring and waved us out of our corners. I came forward and nodded at Cooper, who gazed away at the ceiling, looking profoundly bored. Washington said the usual about protecting yourself at all times, and he crossed to a neutral corner. I went to my corner, the bell rang as I got there, and I turned to find Cooper almost on top of me. He hit me with three quick jabs, moved to my left, and tried a right hook. It missed, thank God, but I was immediately on the defensive. He crowded me toward the ropes, and I tried jabbing and backpedaling toward the center of the ring. But I missed the third jab, went slightly off balance, and was just hanging there when he brought the looping right. I went down sideways to one knee and knelt there stunned. Sergeant Washington jumped between us, put his hands up, and said, "That's it. I overmatched you, boy."

"The hell you did," I said, ducking under his left arm and going straight at Cooper. He got his hands up and tried moving left, but I was already there with the overhand right—what my father used to call the "Dempsey fallaway." Cooper covered but I got the point of the chin, and down he went. He immediately pulled himself on the top rope, just stood there, looking at me and saying: "Jesus Christ, man."

Sergeant Washington jumped between us again, shouting: "All right! That's all! Hit the showers!" He grabbed me by one hand, pulled me toward my corner. "You best come back tomorrow, boy. You need some work on that jab." But he looked pleased, almost smiling.

It hadn't been much of a fight, but I felt exhausted, and stood in the shower until the room was full of steam. The place was empty. No sign of Cooper. He probably hadn't broken a sweat. Then it dawned on me that I was in the "white" shower: the services hadn't been integrated yet, and I was the only damned white man in the gym. And I was standing there considering this when I realized I wasn't alone after all.

Just beyond the cloud of steam, looking ominous in their shoulder-to-shoulder silence, stood four naked black men staring at me stony-eyed. I recognized Cooper, and I thought: Lord, I believe I'm about to pay you an extended visit. And I was sort of looking around for a convenient door or window when Chapman, the heavyweight, appeared to smile. He had arms like gathered cables, but a gentle face. I took the plunge.

"Plenty of room in here, if you're looking to shower."

Silence. Then one of the smaller men spoke. "We already done that. We just wanted to get a good look at you."

"What's your name?" Cooper said.

"Madden. Cully Madden."

"Cully." Cooper absorbed it. Then: "Where'd you learn to hit like that?"

"Home."

"*Home*? Where the hell you live? Madison Square Garden?"

All were smiling now, even chuckling. I let out a blast of relieved air. They hadn't come to wax me after all.

"I'm from New York." I said. "Upstate."

"Ain't he pretty?" one of them said.

"You come to stick?" said the other unknown.

"Stick?"

"He mean stick around," Chappie said. "You goin' to hang with the boxin' team?"

"Well, sure," I said. "If I make the team."

"You make it," Cooper said. "You got it made if you promise to hang in there."

"Is that for you to say?"

"That's right," Cooper said. "Wash let us say who stays and who goes."

"Okay. If you're taking me on, I promise to stick."

"Yeah," one said. "We need us a white boy."

"Get us in the front door," Coop said.

"What front door?"

"Any damn front door, out in the real world. Where black folks ain't always welcome."

"He mean when we on the road," Chappie said. "Specially down in Tennessee and Mississippi and the like, we ain't too welcome sometimes in restaurants and *mo*-tels. You can get us in the front door anyways."

"Fine," I said. "I'll be glad to do that. But I also got to be able to fight."

"You fight fine," Cooper said. "I wouldn't shine you on."

"Okay," I said.

"Come on," Cooper said. "We show you your locker."

Sergeant Kingdom presided over the commissioning of my locker. With the five of us looking on, Sergeant Kingdom took objects from a rubbing table in the aisle of lockers, identified each object aloud (reading from his clipboard), checked the object off, and placed it in the open locker. It was a ritual of some solemnity, no doubt of it, and Sergeant Kingdom observed the proprieties.

"One headgear, leather, size medium," Sergeant Kingdom intoned. Headgear into locker. "One pair boxing shoes, leather, size ten." He turned to me, "I got your size from your sneakers." Into the locker with the shoes. "Two jock straps with cup snaps, size medium." Into the locker. "One athletic cup, O.S.F.A."

"What's that?"

"One size fits all."

The appointing of the locker went on, with styptic, Vaseline, wintergreen oil, rubbing alcohol, Ace bandages, adhesive tape, towels, and iodine. At last came some athletic socks, trunks, tank top shirts, and a brand new mouthpiece.

"Thank you, Sergeant," I said.

"Sign here."

I looked at the form. At the top of the list was one bathrobe, which I hadn't gotten. "What about the bathrobe?"

"You get one soon as the order comes in from St. Louis."

"Right. Thank you." I signed.

Sergeant Kingdom took back his clipboard. "I wish you all the luck," he said. "We damn sure need us a middleweight."

"I'll do my best."

"One last thing." He handed me a padlock and key. "Don't lose the key."

"I won't."

"God bless your white head."

"And God bless yours."

Sergeant Kingdom rubbed his white hair. "Wise ass," he muttered, and moved off down the aisle. Ceremony over.

"Hey!" Chappie said. "You now official."

"But," I said, "I haven't fought any eliminations yet."

"Hell you ain't," said Cooper.

"You all 'liminated," said one.

"Nobody knocks Coop down," Chappie said. "C'mon, we buy you a Coke."

The Fourth Area PX was four tables and two garbage cans, with Fats Waller singing from the juke box. Cooper undertook introductions as soon as we sat down.

"This here's Mr. Chapman, our heavyweight. Mr. Mose Oates, our junior middleweight. And Mr. Waldo Waldron, our welter."

I nodded around at all of them, grinning. Mose looked like forty miles of bad road, with pothole eyes and a sad white-line smile. Waldo was a cutup, a joker with a handsome face, perfect teeth, and a tap dance manner that kept him just ahead of grim realities. Chappie was a sweet-natured bull, eager to listen, easy to laugh. I liked them all. "That's the top half," Cooper said. "You meet the bottom half tomorrow. They's Sonny Bliss, lightweight. Stone the feather. And Spider Webb the bantam."

"We got no fly," Waldo said. "Doin' without one. But Coop's got the fastest fly in the Air Force."

Coop sprayed Waldo with Coke, and Waldo managed to spray the rest of us. The fight got serious and Chappie and I were left alone.

"So, your name's Charlie?"

"Cully."

"New one on me."

"It's Irish. I got it from a great-grandfather."

"You stationed here?"

"Yeah. Aren't you?"

"No, I'm on TDY, from Elmendorf in Alaska. Just got there, had to turn around and come here. Most of us are in from other bases for eliminations."

"Elmendorf? Where's that?"

"Anchorage, Alaska. Hell, Waldo, he came in from Japan. And Mose from Guam, I think. And Coop, he was in Okee-bokee. Somethin' like that."

"Okinawa," Cooper said, rejoining us. "I was in charge of beach detail. Pickin' up old bones and bullets. Glad to get out of there." The other two, soaked from the waist up with cola spray, also sat down, wiping at themselves and their grins with napkins. "I used to be a corporal."

"What happened?"

"Oh, I hit a candy ass who was foolin' with my girl."

"He was a staff sergeant," Chappie said. "With wings."

"He was a bird-dog," Coop said. "Now he got false teeth."

Chappie pointed at me. "He's based here."

"Doing *what*?" Mose asked.

"School. Cryptography school."

"What's that?"

"Codes and ciphers."

"That's secret stuff?" Coop asked.

"They think so."

"When do you finish?"

"In three weeks."

"That's perfect," Coop said. "We got our first big fight three weeks from tomorrow."

"In East Saint," Waldo said.

"East Saint Louis?" I said. "Isn't that off limits?"

"It oughta be off the map," Chappie said. "Toughest damn town in America, what I hear."

"We goin' to get a *po*-lice escort into the ring," Waldo said.

"We're goin' to need it," Chappie said.

"I doubt I'll be in shape by then," I said to Cooper.

"Don't worry," Waldo said. "They goin' to shoot us anyways."

"You be in shape," Coop said. "I'll make sure."

"Okay," I said. "And I'll make sure you are."

"Fair enough," Cooper said.

Chappie leaned to me. "You think you're okay to fight us a couple of eliminations tomorrow?"

"We're still fighting eliminations?"

"Sure. They still sendin' in turkeys from all over. We got twenty, twenty-five of them left."

"Well, hell, I'll give it my best shot. Help get me ready."

"You're ready, Mr. Madden," Cooper said.

"Thank you, Mr. Cooper."

"You're welcome," he said, grinning. "And call me Coop."

Dickess was stretched out on his bunk when I got back to the barracks.

"Hey," he said. "I thought you was in the stockade!"

"Keep thinking that, Dickess. And you'll be as right as you usually are."

"Then I was up to the orderly room, and I heard all this shit about the boxing team."

"Ridiculous," I said. "Totally unfounded rumor."

"Well, that's what I say," he said, flopping back on his pillow. "I said Madden's crazy, but even he ain't that crazy. I mean, they're all niggers, you know. Every one a nigger, they say. I asked around. All niggers. And stink? Lordy Jesus!"

I had to hold onto my bedstead to keep from going at him. And I was thinking: Lord, You must have had some good awful reason for putting Dickess among us. I pray that You communicate this to me, preferably within the next twenty-four hours, or I'm afraid that I'll be forced to murder the son-of-a-bitch.

FOUR

You gon' keep on monkeyin' 'round here friend-boy.
You gon' get your
business all in a trick.

Robert Johnson, "Sweet Home Chicago"

I got word the next morning that I was to take my meals henceforth at the Fourth Area mess. Corporal Culpepper, who was from somewhere south of south, delivered the news with something close to utter disbelief.

"Madden here?"

"Yo."

"Madden, I got me a paper from the colonel says that, from now on, you eat at the black mess. Over in the Fourth?"

"Starting today?"

"At dinner. You eat dinner and supper there? Seems like they got a training table?" He looked at me blinking. "What the hell this all about, Madden?"

"The boxing team."

"The Niggra boxing team?"

"The Air Force boxing team."

"The hell you say. We goin' to have us a black boxing team?"

"Well, I'll be on it, by the looks."

"Well, you just might be, but that don't make it right, does it? I mean, shitfire!"

He looked so distressed that I almost laughed. "You can come over with me and try out, Corporal."

There was laughter in the ranks.

"You think I'd sit down and eat with them people? That'd be the goddamn day!" He wadded up the colonel's message and tossed it to one side. "Okay, Madden. I'm goin' to keep my eye on you. You start suckin' on watermelon rinds, you're out of my barracks."

I felt, then, like telling him he was a cracker horse's ass, but I was in enough trouble already.

The Fourth Area mess hall was a surprisingly well-kept mess, but I don't think I really noticed that at first. I'd spent all morning at the cryptography school trying to crack a German World War I code. My assigned partner was a very bright kid named Levitt from Chicago, who seemed entranced with the whole cryptographic bollix. He would stick his head in at whatever machine we were using (probably the M-209) so that I couldn't see a damn thing and then rise up and ask me what I thought. What I thought was that he would likely make a great cryptanalyst, and I wished him well.

"But I mean, what do you think of the problem?"

"How the hell do I know? I can't see through your fat head."

He would take offense but not the hint, and he kept right on until, in fact, we cracked the code—the first pair in our class—and while I took some small satisfaction, I claimed no credit. It was all Levitt, and I was very sad to hear, some time later, that he had been discharged on a Section Eight or some such, for exposing himself on the streets of Belleville, Illinois, and peeing all over a floral display at a Jewish wedding. What he was doing there I don't know, except that I do remember he was excessively fond of lox.

There were two chow lines stretching from the back of the mess hall to the front. I got into one of them and was being openly stared at by all (being, of course, the only white face in the vicinity), when I heard:

"Hey, white boy!"

I looked around and there, thank God, was Cooper.

"What do you want, black boy?" I said softly.

"Watch your mouth," Cooper said. "You want to get yourself peeled?"

He took me by the arm, led me off down toward the front of the hall, then over to one side, to a large table set apart from the others. There, seated, were Chappie, Waldo, Mose, and Sergeants Washington and Kingdom at either end of the table. There were three others, whom I rightly assumed were the other members of the team. All were eating, and all looked up when Sergeant Washington said: "Well, here's my middle man."

"Sergeant," I said, nodding.

"Got some people here you don't know yet." He stood up. "First off, this here's Cully Madden, our middleweight."

"Unless, of course," said Cooper, "somebody takes him out."

Wash ignored him. "Now, this here's Dee-Wayne Bliss. Sonny. Lightweight. And this here's Bobby Ray Livingstone. Stone. Featherweight. And this here's Tree-maine Webb, Spider-ass. Bantam."

Each rose as he was introduced, shook my hand somewhat solemnly, then grinned and sat down. Coop ushered me toward a seat. I looked toward the serving table just beyond the head of the table.

"Don't we get trays, and—"

"No, no," Coop said, smiling. "We got waiters."

And indeed we did: two guys in white, who served me a hamburger steak, medium rare, and gravy, mashed potatoes, and green beans. And even got me a carton of milk when I asked for it. I looked at Coop, after a moment, and found him grinning at me.

"High on the hog, ain't it? Old Wash's got in-*flu*-ence."

One of the waiters set down a plate with a piece of pie on it, covered with whipped cream. I looked at Coop. "My God," I said.

"Apple pie," Coop said. "Good for the bowel."

I had finished everything, and was halfway through the pie—which was delicious, the first real dessert I'd had since signing up—when Washington got to his feet and dinged on a metal water pitcher with a knife.

"Okay. Hear me, people." He consulted a note. "We got exactly thirty-two casuals need eliminatin'. You each take two a afternoon, we be clear by Friday." Another look at the note. "One problem. We got six heavies. 'Specially them two from Samoa or what the hell. So, Chappie, you get three. Cooper gets two. And, Madden, you think you could handle a heavy?"

"I'll try," I said.

"He be fine," Coop said.

"That's settle," Washington said. "Now, none of them look prime to me. But gotta warn you again . . . you lose two fights, you go on reserve. You get a rematch, but you'd best win it." He shrugged. "All up to you. But I tell you now . . . *this* my team. Don't frig me over."

He stood looking at us for a moment, then quickly blessed himself. And my first meal was over. I looked at Coop.

"Good God. It can't be that cut and dried."

"Why not?" Coop said. "Wash tell it like it is. Every time out. He got the Air Force by the left tit. Believe it."

My first fight was not with a heavyweight, but a light heavy at most, who was in from Great Falls, Montana. He was cocky, well-muscled, and, as it turned out, fast. He threw me a couple of rapid jabs, looked annoyed when I blocked them, and looked positively astonished when I hit him with a routine right hand. I just boxed him for the first round. When I got to the corner, Wash was glowering at me.

"What the hell you doin'?"

"Boxing."

"Who the hell ask you to box? Hit him, and hit him hard."

"I might hurt him, Sergeant."

"Then hurt him! Kid's got to learn he could get hisself killed, fartin' around like he do. Go on, now. Put him down."

"Down? You mean that?"

"Down! Goddamn, Madden, you a little slow on the uptake." Then, as the bell rang, "Put him *down*!"

The opponent obliged me by coming on like Jack Johnson as we got into the second round. He missed about five fierce right hands before I decided to tap him. The next time he came in lunging behind a left hook and started the looping right, I stepped inside the left and, as he threw the right over my shoulder, I brought the right uppercut. He went down hard, flat on his back. I thought to go to him—he was lying there with his mouth wide open and his legs twitching—but I knew Sergeant Washington would land on me if I did, so I walked back to my corner, saying to Wash: "I think he may be hurt."

"Good," Wash said, grinning hugely. "Now he's got something to tell his grandchillun. He got hisself sincerely starched."

I was to find out that "sincerely starched" was one of Wash's favorite expressions. Wash liked everything sincerely starched. When the opponent finally got up, I went over to him and told him that he had done very well. He looked at me wide-eyed, and I knew he wasn't really seeing me and he said: "What the hell was *that*?" And that's all he said. I went back to my corner thinking: I know I've got a good right hand, but not that good. Obviously, the opponent had no chin at all.

Later that day, Coop took on one of the Samoans. A big, beefy man with legs like a baby elephant. Coop could hit him at will, and, since he was pouring sweat almost immediately, each shot raised a geyser of perspiration that showered even the ringsiders.

I was working the corner with Wash. That means I was in charge of putting the stool and water bucket into the ring between rounds. Spider was working the other corner, and had a towel over his head against the sweat storms. I knew the thing couldn't last. About halfway through the first round, Coop, clutched up in what must have been the thirty-second clinch, looked over the Samoan's shoulder and shouted to Wash: "You going to call this off?"

"I ain't callin' nothin'!" Wash shouted back, somewhat annoyed.

"Aw, for Christ's sake," Coop said.

"Never mind Christ! Tend to business!"

Coop pushed off the Samoan, frowned ferociously at Wash, put his right hand behind his back and proceeded to dance around the Samoan like a matador around a bull, whacking him with left hands. Wash let out a roar: "Hot damn you, fight!"

Coop looked at Wash with something like disdain, and tended to business. The final shot was a walk-by left that stopped the Samoan's head while his feet walked right out from under it. The Samoan went down on the end of his spine with his feet kicking in the air. He issued a great gasp, his heels came down on the canvas like a couple of pistons, and he was still. Coop came over to the corner, spit out his mouthpiece, and said: "There you are, Sergeant."

Wash glowered at him: "If I had time, and didn't need you, I'd whup your showboat-ass! Don't you ever—*ever*—showboat around again like that, you hear?"

Wash's anger was intimidating, even to Coop, but he still managed to shout: "Yes, *sir*!" with distinct sarcasm as he leapt from the ring and trotted toward the showers.

Wash stared after him. "That boy's got a big gift. And I'm goin' to give him another one some of these days. A swift kick in his fancy ass."

It took twenty minutes to revive the Samoan.

My heavyweight looked like a very large hawk—about two hundred pounds of hawk—maybe one axe-handle across the shoulders and a gaze pitiless as the sun. When Wash came back from talking to him in the far corner, he said: "I don't know about this one. Says he a Indian, and that he fought a couple of prelims in Walla Walla. For a lumber company." He paused, looked back across the ring. "You'd best whomp on his arms for awhile."

"You'd best find me a crowbar," I said.

"Just be artful," Wash said.

The big man came out of his corner in a sort of rapid stutter-step behind a stiffly extended left glove. When he got close enough to me he flopped the left back and forth, and then unleased a mighty right hand. I felt the damned breeze, which at the time was welcome. I moved in, pushed him off. And to my astonishment he staggered backward and, literally, fell on his butt in front of Wash. I looked at Wash, who was looking at me, and he spoke sharply: "Don't look at me, Madden! Stoke it to him!"

"Wash, for God's sake. He couldn't hit a bull in the ass with a snow shovel!"

"Damn you, Madden! Do like I say!"

While I was still looking at Wash, the Indian, who had gotten to his feet, hit me a shot in the throat. He could hit. I turned around and addressed myself to the problem. He was not, as one might say, a shrinking violet. He came right at me, windmilling punches. I backed away for a moment, then hit him right on the nose with three quick jabs. He came to a half-stop, then threw the biggest right hand he could muster. I slipped it, moved to the left, came back in with a leaning right hand that caught him full in the mouth. He stopped short, pop-eyed, and I drove two lefts to his belly-button. He snorted loudly, doubled over, spat out his mouthpiece, and came up holding both hands high in surrender.

"That don't feel so good," he said.

"Well, Jesus, I'm sorry."

"That's enough. Thank you, sir."

And, brushing past me as he headed to his corner, he departed the ring with entire dignity, as if he had been violated and would no longer grace the premises with his presence.

I went back to Wash, who was grinning but trying to cover it.

"What do you make of that?"

"Man ain't got the balls for it," Wash said. "Chappie would have killed him."

"Well, pardon me, Wash. I hope I didn't ruin your afternoon."

Wash smiled at me, almost fondly. "You somethin' else, at your one hundred sixty pounds," he said. "But we already got us enough wise-ass with Mr. Cooper."

"He's our best."

"Don't you tell him that."

"I don't have to. He knows."

Wash cocked his chin at me. "What makes you think you know anything about the ring?"

"My father taught me what I know."

"Your father?"

"He was a heavyweight. Fought his way through Fordham Law School. At the old Saint Nick's arena. In New York."

"I'll be damned. Well, he taught you good. But you just remember, you ain't no heavyweight. You keep on fightin' like one, somebody's going to take your head off."

"I'll bear that in mind."

"You do that, boy."

That night we had real beefsteak for dinner. I could not by God believe it. I hadn't had a steak since I left the farm. When I ordered mine extra rare, Wash said: "That the way, Madden. This here's prime stuff. I got it sent in special from Saint Louis."

"Thank you, Sergeant."

"Going to be first class from here on out," he said. "Long's the money come to hand."

Later, Wash stood up, dinged the water pitcher, and gave us our marching orders. "I got something to say I didn't want to say until the team was final. So open your ear holes. Now, we fight, like I said, in East Saint on Saturday night. And we stay in a hotel that night, and Sunday morning we head south. I got us two Hudson Hornet automobiles, damn near brand new. Staff cars, they are, for officers. But I got them from the colonel because we are going to travel in style."

Coop started to applaud, and the rest of us joined in. Wash looked pleased.

"Where we're going to end up is Biloxi, Mississippi, where we going to fight the United States Marines in the quarterfinals."

"For God's sake," I said. "We are?"

"Damn right. But we going to be fighting all the way down. First stop is Cape Girardeau, Missouri, and we got a fight there Sunday night. Then New Madrid, Memphis, Vicksburg, Natchez, Baton Rouge, and New Iberia, Louisiana, just upstreet of where I was born."

We all clapped again. Wash held up one hand.

"We got us two fights in New Orleans. So by the time we get out to Biloxi, we ought to be in pretty damn good fighting rig."

We were quiet. We weren't so damned sure.

"All this has been arranged by friends of mine—managers and promoters—and nothing is wrote on stone. But I can vouch for most of it. No real money, but enough so we eat good."

"Sergeant?" Chappie said.

"Yeah?"

"We fightin' quarterfinals? I mean, we ain't fought dip-diddle yet, and we fightin' quarterfinals?"

"Well, goddamn, Chappie, there's the Army, the Navy, the

Marines and the Air Force. That's four. You going to have quarterfinals, you got to have four. I mean, they's four quarters to any damn thing!"

Chappie looked quashed, so I broke in: "But the other services have all had their own eliminations? Marine teams against Marines . . . and so on? And we're going to fight the best team all those marines could produce?"

"That's right, Madden. You want out?"

"Hell no," I said. "I like our chances. I think."

"You hang onto that thought, Madden. You going to need it. We all alone, I grant you that. But we be tough and tougher. And the Air Force is banking on us. I mean, people, we are the official *it*."

We all applauded again, and, for the first time, I felt conjoined, bolstered. I just might survive the goddamned Air Force after all.

FIVE

Mr. Highwayman
Plea-hease don't block the road.

Robert Johnson, "Terraplane Blues"

The next morning, I said goodbye to Dickess. The dumb bastard just couldn't keep his mouth shut. I was packing my duffel bag, putting in everything but a class A uniform and shoes (which I would wear), when he came up behind me and said, "Jigaboo!"

I almost wheeled on him, but I held back with some effort. "Dickess, you horse's ass, have you a death wish?"

"Just saying goodbye," he said.

"And you think that's a proper goodbye?"

"Well, you're going to come back at least half jigaboo, right?"

I set myself, turned, and hit him one of the sweetest right hands I've ever thrown. He seemed to come off the floor a bit, and went backward clear across the middle of the bay, skidded across the top of a bunk, and socked into the far wall so hard I thought he might have broken his neck.

"Jesus Christ!" he said, and then passed out.

I didn't look at him or go to him. Morton assured me I had killed him. What would I have done without Morton to report exigent mortalities?

I said, "Pour some water on the son-of-a-bitch. If he doesn't wake up in twenty-four hours, call a mortician."

And I picked up my duffel bag and went out.

The staging area was the front of the Fourth Area gym. I was the last to arrive, but Coop had saved space for my bag in the trunk of the lead car.

"You get to ride up front," Coop said. "I be right behind you."

"Well, thank you, Coop."

"Don't thank him," Wash said. "I appointed you navigator, because you're the only one around here seem to know where he's going."

"Who's that?" I asked, pointing to a young officer, a second lieutenant, who was stuffing his B-4 bag into the trunk of the second car.

"Name's March," said Wash. "They figured we needed a white officer. I don't want him, I don't like him, but we got him."

"Does he fight?"

"No. He a track man. He can run like hell."

"Well," I said, "he might be useful."

"He can run ahead of us and arrange the publicity," Coop said.

Wash looked at him with his mouth pursed up against a laugh. But then he let it go: wahooing, slapping his thighs, walking quick-step through a full circle. Then he stopped, got out his handkerchief, and was wiping his eyes when Lieutenant March came over.

"Sergeant? I think we're running a little behind schedule."

"Well," Wash said, barely able to hold his composure, "If you start running now, sir, we do our best to catch up."

"What was that? Do you have some idea I'm going to run ahead of the cars? Are you serious?"

Wash exploded in more laughter, absolutely overcome, and staggered away and fell to his knees in helpless glee.

Lieutenant March looked at him sourly. I jumped in. "The sergeant has had some bad news," I said. "He's not quite himself."

"I certainly hope not," March said. "We have a rigorous journey ahead of us."

"Yes, sir," I said.

"And what is your name?" he asked, looking me up and down.

"Catfish Madden," I said, straight-faced.

March nodded dubiously. "Some of you have the strangest names."

March walked away.

Wash had heard me, and it took fully ten minutes to get him to stop snuffling and get to his feet.

"Well, Catfish," he said. "Break out the fucking maps and saddle up. We going to a track meet."

And finally we were on the road, State Route 59, a two-lane blacktop from Belleville to East St. Louis. Our Hudson Hornets were very impressive, still smelled new, and accommodated us nicely. I sat in the front of the lead car with Wash, a stack of road maps between us. I had my window open, my right hand up on the roof, thoroughly enjoying the day, the breeze, and the freedom. Wash had Blind Boy Fuller's "Rag, Mama, Rag" on the radio, loud, and Cooper and Chappie were both singing along in the back seat. I felt emancipated. I'd graduated first in my class from crypto school (much to my surprise and Levitt's consternation), and I was dropping the world of five-letter groups behind me like a turdweight. We were off on a great adventure on the fertile breast of the American continent, and there was nothing for it but to exult. I found marvelous pleasure in the fetid air and drab landscape of the road into East Saint. And it wasn't until we'd actually gotten into the wretched, scarred brick slums of the town that my enthusiasm began to wane. I turned to Wash. "Good God, Wash. This place looks like it's been bombed."

"It has, Catfish. And it's still going on."

"Those people staring at us, they look angry."

"They are."

"Why?"

"New cars. They angry at anything new."

"Jesus, Wash. I don't think we ought to stop here."

Wash laughed, as did Coop and Mose. "Oh, it gets better, Madden. It gets much better. Long about eight o'clock tonight." All three laughed—dark, barrel-room black laughter.

We pulled up in front of a red brick blight of a hotel. Wash got out and immediately encountered a burly man with an eye patch on the left side.

"Hey, Wash."

"Hey, Pie. How they hangin'?"

"Spring plums, man. Gettin' bigger all the time."

Both men laughed as Wash walked past him into the hotel. I got out and stood on the sidewalk as a small crowd began to gather. One of the young men—utter black with yellow eye-whites—eased over toward me. "Hey, white boy. Who the hell you?"

"Boxing team."

He turned and let out a small chorus of derisive laughter.

"You the manager?"

"I'm the middleweight."

More laughter.

"You goin' to fight ours tonight?"

"That's the rumor."

"You goin' to die, boy. Right here in East Saint."

Coop and Chappie got out and moved up on either side of me. "Go on in," Coop said to me softly. "I bring your bags."

I almost ran into the hotel, with Lieutenant March right behind me. The desk clerk, a small man with steel-rimmed glasses, was talking: "You want to put the two white men in together?"

"What did he say?" Lieutenant March said.

"He say," Wash said, "you want Madden in with you?"

"An enlisted man?" March said.

Coop, just coming through the door, said, "Put him in with me."

Wash looked at the desk clerk: "Do it."

Lieutenant March stared off into midair, and I don't think I have ever disliked another human being so intensely on such short acquaintance.

The place smelled of decay, slow dying. I stood at the window staring out at the dismal city. Coop was stretched out on one of the single beds.

"Tough-looking town," I said.

"Armpit of Illinois."

"Is it going to get any better?"

"Oh, yeah, it's on its way to being the crotch of Illinois."

"No, I mean, as we go south."

"You kiddin'? You ever hear of New Orleans?"

"I've seen pictures. Looks great."

"You talkin' about heaven. My hometown. And just wait till you see Lainie."

"Lainie?"

"My girl! Hey, I got a picture." He started for his wallet, then stopped. "No. You too young. For *this* picture."

"I'm eighteen, as old as you are."

Coop shook his head, grinned. "You ain't never goin' to be as old as I am."

"What's that mean?"

"Oh, I seen you prayin'. Before you eat, after you eat. Before you crap, after you crap. Prayin' don't jive with growin' up."

"Maybe you'd rather I didn't room with you?"

"Oh, it's okay." A big grin. "Long's you sleep on the floor."

The East Saint Boxing Club had taken over a small movie theater for the night. From the smell and shab of it, it probably hadn't shown a movie in fifteen years. The ring was set up just in front of the movie screen, and the ring posts were square, heavy metal, which no doubt reached straight through the floor into the ground beneath. Somehow this worried me. We came in through a side door and were immediately met by an ululation of catcalls, boos, insults, obscenities, and general vituperation that, literally, shocked me. I mean, here we were, dressed in the class A uniforms of our country's air service, and overwhelmingly black, and guests in the place, and they greet us like we were the German army. I got used to this sort of thing after a while, but it was only later that I figured out that the very nature of boxing—the fight to the death with all your soul hanging out—provokes the most primitive emotions, reduces civilization to an irrelevance.

There were ten East Saint cops going through the motions, and we pushed them ahead of us toward the dressing room. The impression I got from that perilous passage through the crowd was of faces leaning in at us—snarling, twisted faces, with teeth bared and eyes with an intensity of hate and violence that I'd never seen before. And some of those faces were of women—some of them quite beautiful—but with massacred lipstick and teeth bared and jawbones set to chew your face off.

We had almost made it to the dressing room when somebody took a swing at Chappie, who was leading the charge. Chappie swung back, removing most of the front teeth of a man twice his size. Uproar, screams, and howls of outrage, and it was about to get entirely out of hand when there came an overmanning bellow from Wash. "Hey, you police cops! Get them niggers out of the way!"

The use of the word "niggers" had a strange effect. If a white man had used it, I'm sure he would have been disemboweled on the spot. But a very large black man, covered with ribbons and stripes of rank, had used it, and it caused a sudden quiet, a falling back, an atavistic reaction to a powerful voice of authority. When I asked Coop about it later, he said, "Well, they were *acting* like niggers, and Wash made them realize it. No big thing." Maybe it wasn't to Coop, but it was to me, and it took weeks before I began to understand it.

The dressing room was a low-ceilinged cavern under the stage. The East Saint team was at one end of the room, the Air Force at the other. Nothing in between. The East Saint team was entirely black, hard-bodied—much like the men on our team. With one striking difference: the hairdos. Afros, braids, frizzes, giving them a fiercer, wilder look than we could command.

"They look mean," I said to Coop.

"Never mind them. You see that poontang?"

Wash overheard. "Never mind the goddamn poontang, Cooper! You mess with their women, you find your black ass hung!"

"Already hung," Coop whispered to me, flashing a grin. "That's my whole damn problem."

The East Saint manager—the man named Pie—came over to watch while Wash wrapped our hands. After a moment, he said, "We can weigh them now if you want to."

"Hell, I trust you, Pie," Wash said. "But let me see your feather."

Pie turned, shouted: "Hey, Kisser! Over here!"

Kisser, a wild-eyed, wild-haired, scrawny-hard kid, stepped into the neutral zone and pursed his lips belligerently.

"He look about right," Wash said.

"*Kisser*!" Stone said with a shake of his head.

"Kiss my ass!" Kisser said.

"I'll bust it for you!" Stone said, half-rising.

Outcries on both sides until Pie shouted at his team, "Shut your goddamn faces!"

Wash chucked Stone under the chin. "As you was! You get your chance."

I didn't get to see the Stone-Kisser fight, but I could hear it, especially the stomping of feet that shook the whole building. Kisser won on points, and I was up next. Coop was sitting next to me, and pointed to my opponent, wearing an Afro, a yellow robe, and following his trainer out with his hands on the trainer's shoulders.

"Looks ready," Coop said.

"Looks tough," I said.

"Naw. Just hit him where he lives. In the hairdo."

Lieutenant March, who had just managed to sneak in from the cars, spoke to me from the door. "Okay, Madden. You're up."

At the door, I met Stone coming in. "Jesus, Cully. Watch the women. One poked me in the eye. And I *lost*!"

We eased out into the crowd, March flanked by two policemen, and two more flanking me. The crowd was watching something going on in the ring—some kind of girly show—so they didn't notice us until we were almost there. But then the hoots and snarls started, and the four cops closed in and almost lifted me up onto the ring apron. Wash reached out and hauled me between the ropes to the stool.

"You okay?"

"Yeah."

"Come on," he said, as he pulled me up and we crossed to the resin box. I could barely hear him over the crowd noise as he went on. "Seen this boy last year! Like to turn and walk away from you now and then. He do that, climb his back! Coldcock him! You hear me?"

"I hear you."

I did the resin, came back to my corner. The animosity and vitriol from the crowd was unrelieved. I just told myself that my white skin was all I had to live in, and if they didn't like it, why that was just too goddamned bad.

When the bell rang, I came off the stool and ran into a stiff left jab. Followed by a right to the belt-line that really hurt. I backed away, considered my opponent. He had a wild look in his eye, but he was not physically much better off than I was. I moved in, hit him with a swatting right to his left side, followed by two left hooks, and a closing overhand right. He stopped almost still, and I knew I had gotten some respect. Then he suddenly turned and walked away from me—such an arrogant, full-back walkaway that I was temporarily stunned.

Wash shouted: "Climb his ass!"

Yes, sir, I thought. And moved to do so. But just as I got close, he turned to meet me. I jabbed, moved back, and he came on quickly and hit me a hard shot in the throat. I thought he had sauced my Adam's apple, and I damned near went down. But I tucked my chin, hauled on the larnyx, got steady again, and, as he came in, hit him with a right hook, driving him back. I was having trouble breathing, but I pursued, and, just as I was about to start a combination, he turned and walked off again. Full back to me. I didn't need Wash this time. I leaped after him, hit him a gathered left on one side, and, as he half-turned, brought the full overhand right. He went down like a sledge-hammered ox and didn't so much as twitch.

There was an instant of stunned silence, and then the place erupted in outrage. I'd hit him from behind! Foul! Foul most foul! Kill the son-of-a-bitch! And so on. Six cops jumped into the ring, surrounded me, and with Wash's assistance got me off the apron and into the mob. I noticed the referee finishing the count as we left, and then we walked into it: a sea of open mouths, shaking fists, hate-filled eyes. We were almost clear of the mob when a woman with orange hair broke past two of the cops, swung her handbag, and hit me in the head. There must have been a brick in the damned thing. I started to sag, but the cops held me up, and we finally made the dressing room. I looked at Waldo, who was up next, and said, "Waldo, if you value your life, don't go out there."

Waldo looked at me sadly. "Well, Cully, I ain't got much value on it, you get right down to it."

And I remember thinking: Jesus God, this madness is institutionalized. They think it's the normal conduct of pugilistic business.

And, as the trip wore on, I discovered that I was absolutely right.

It happened that I was with Wash the next morning when we met with Pie to discuss the night's business. We had won four, lost four, and Wash was in no mood to be affable. "I need a witness," he said, as we drew up in front of Pie's place, which was a black shack bar out of James Agee by Walker Evans.

"If I hit him," Wash said, "remember exactly what you saw."

"I will."

We went in, to a back table, where Pie was waiting. We were eyed balefully by bartender and several dissolute-looking customers.

Pie was sorting among ten and twenty dollar bills. He looked up. Then he pushed a pile of bills—a small pile—at Wash as we sat down. "I got expenses," Pie said.

Wash thumbed through the money. Then, "Little light, Pie."

"I say I got expenses."

"I know your expenses," Wash said. "And I also counted the house."

Pie shrugged. "Man's got to live."

"I'm lookin' at a long, dry road, Pie."

"You got government money," Pie said.

"I got gas and meal allowance that don't make it by half," Wash said. "You know the drill."

Pie said, "How about forty more?"

"How about eighty?"

Pie shook his head sadly from side to side, then picked up the roll and stripped off three bills. “Here’s sixty,” Pie said. “That cuts me to the nut.”

Wash shook his head dubiously. Then reached over, snatched another ten from Pie’s roll. “Now,” he said, “now we’s close to even.”

Pie shrugged again. “You takin’ a man’s livelihood.”

Wash smiled. “Keep you mean and slender.”

Pie nodded, almost smiled. “So, you goin’ home?”

“New Iberia,” Wash said, “God willin’ and the crick stays down.”

“That real South,” Pie said. “Hit me on the way back?”

Wash nods. “If I got anythin’ left to hit with.”

Pie nodded, Wash nodded, and I simply stared. Then Wash pushed me with an elbow in the near ribs, and I jumped to my feet, suffused with revelation about how things were done in the real boxing business.

SIX

I'll pack my trunk,
Make ma get away.

W. C. Handy, "St. Louis Blues"

We were finally free of the North and headed the Hudsons south along old Route 61, the road into the great American mystery of the South, with everybody in our car singing while Chappie rippled out the chords of Huddie Ledbetter's "Irene." And we were hurting—Chappie more than anybody after a low-down, mean fight with a ball-bashing son-of-a-bitch who had the most talented right kneelift seen since Harry Greb. But we were joyous, going into home country, home for most of us, and ripe and ready as young lions for whatever the hell lay ahead.

Wash had managed to find me beat-up copies of the WPA Writer's Project manuals for Missouri, Tennessee, Mississippi, and Louisiana, so that I was equipped to comment on passing highlights such as the old St. Louis courthouse where Dred Scott first presented his case. Nobody knew who Dred Scott was except Tremaine, and I was trying to bring the others up to speed when Chappie twelve-stringed me into song.

-45-

When we had calmed down a little, Wash tried to prepare us somewhat for the evening. Cape Girardeau was a quiet little river town for sure, but the manager there was ambitious, and had got himself a pretty fair team together, with an eye on the state championship. He was particular in what he took for his team, and Wash said he expected "a good test." We would be fighting, from what he understood, on a big river barge moored at the local locks. The light was sure to be bad to indifferent, so there was to be no messing around, because any goddamned thing can happen in the dark, and the benefit of any doubt was sure to go to the home team. I expected Wash to get around to "sincerely starched," but he knew we were hurting a bit and spared us. He told me to be sure that the people in the other car got the word.

I should explain the traveling arrangements. Wash drove the lead car with me in the front seat to navigate and receive and disseminate bulletins from the pilot's seat. In the backseat were Chappie, Coop, and Sonny. The second car had Ace Kingdom driving with Lieutenant March and Spider in the front seat with him. Stone, Waldo, and Mose occupied the backseat. These arrangements were regularly varied because nobody wanted to ride with March, especially when he took the wheel—he drove like an old lady, often falling well behind our car so that we had to pull over and wait for him to catch up. So the first-cabin people would sometimes take mercy on the second-cabin people and swap places for a day. But it was considered hard time, and neither Coop nor I ever participated.

The road ran through mostly dairy pasture with an occasional corn or soybean spread, and at first it looked neat and prosperous, but there was no question that poverty was steadily setting in, the farther south we went.

Cape Girardeau was maybe the last really high point, with broad streets, big houses neatly kept, and front yards full of perfectly clipped emphatically green grass. There was a big beige-bricked Catholic church with an impressive white spire, a Boatmen's Bank, and the levee just down the street from our hotel. Most impressive were the huge iron gates that the Corps of Engineers had begun to construct after the great flood of 1927. High-water marks—1844, 1943—were painted in black, with, away up at the top, fully twenty feet off the ground, block letters saying: POSSIBLE HIGH WATER. Having been brought up on the peaceful Hudson, I found these gates more than somewhat disturbing. What the hell did people live here for, when the river was so obviously the enemy? But you couldn't be there long before you knew why people lived there: it was a handsome town, beautiful in its trees and orderliness, and beautiful in its determination to live with the damned river as one might live with an irascible, foul-tempered grandfather.

Our hotel, as I said, was a short block from the levee and the great iron gates. As we pulled up, Sonny said, "We going to eat lunch?"

"Yeah."

"I think I saw a fried-chicken place, just up the hill."

"No chicken for you. You fightin' tonight. You eatin' beefsteak."

"Beefsteak. Again?"

The whole car broke out in laughter.

The hotel was black-run, solid red brick, clean. The team gathered at the front desk, all except Lieutenant March, who, after the bags were unloaded, took off in the second car to find himself a "white" hotel. It happened time and again, and March must have had his own money, because Wash refused to give him an extra nickel.

The clerk said, "Who your middleweight?"

I said, "I am."

"Hee hee," said the clerk.

"What's funny?" I said.

"You find out."

Coop's and my room looked down River Street toward the great hinged floodgates, and when I got up from a nap just after dark I could see the ring set up on the first barge, with floodlights at either end. Spectators were already filing in—blacks to one side, whites to the other three sides, the traditional Southern arrangement. It looked stark, pitiless—a place to die—and I felt a shiver run through me and remembered reading somewhere long ago Calpurnius Flaccus's remark: "There is no meaner condition among the people than that of the gladiator." At that moment, Coop came in and said it was time for me to go down to the lobby and get taped, and I went down thinking: Gladiator, cinch up your loins. We are about to put you to the mortal test.

Less than half an hour later I was looking across the ring at my opponent—a mulatto with a ringlet hairdo and forearms the size of rope fenders. He had already come over to greet me, wild-eyed, saying—or, rather, chanting—that his name was Crazy Dixon. The crowd seemed to love him, and I stood there thinking I must have pissed on an icon somewhere along the line for the gods to be doing this to me.

Sure enough, he came out of his corner, feinted left, fell back right, leaped in, put me in a headlock, and started punching me in the face with his free hand. I looked at the referee, but he seemed to be enjoying the action. Then Wash was at the ropes, beating at the referee with a towel and bellowing for him to do his job and call a foul. The referee frowned and grabbed Crazy by the back of his trunks, and told him to let go of my neck, but you might as well have told a dog to drop the cat. I finally managed to crank myself around and drive my right into his solar plexus. He issued a mighty belch, let go of my neck, stepped back, spit out his mouthpiece, and cried: "Low blow!" I stepped in with the straight right hook and split him down the nose.

Then, my God, you'd have thought I'd violated him with a rusty harpoon. He started full circuits of the ring, splattering blood everywhere, calling on the crowd—which was working up to full frenzy—to observe how it was with him: attacked by a brute with a razor in his glove.

I sort of backed toward our corner, chewed my mouthpiece out of the way, and said: "Wash, this son-of-a-bitch *is* crazy."

"Stick him!" Wash said. "Stick him! Keep him off you!"

"Wash, I'm telling you, call the police. I'm serious. Call the AAU."

Ace said, "He cut you bad! Watch your eyes!"

I could feel the blood running down my face, but at that point the referee caught Crazy, turned him around, and waved me in.

"You! You incompetent jackass!" I shouted at the referee. "Why don't you—"

Which was as far as I got because Crazy ducked under the referee's arm and hit me a first-class shot that deposited me on my back in my corner. The bell rang, and Coop (who'd joined the corner), Wash, and Ace pulled me up on the stool and went to work.

"He bit me!" I said. "He bit my nose!"

"Yep," said Ace. "Tooth marks."

"You going to let this go on, Wash?"

"Got to. Under the contract."

"Screw the contract. He's crazy!"

"Sure. That what they call him."

The bell rang, and here came Crazy charging across the ring

like a mad bull. I swung just as he got to me, but he lowered his head, hit me full in the chest, and down I went again.

"Stay down," Wash shouted. "Stay right there! This fool'll kill ya!"

The referee had already started counting, and I let him reach eight, then I pulled myself on the ropes, turned to Wash. "I am going to hand you his goddamned head!" The referee stepped in and tried to hold me back, but I shoved him out of the way, and went at Crazy. He was standing on the middle strand, waving mildly at the black quarter of the crowd, and the applause and shouting were deafening.

I grabbed him at the waist with both gloves, pulled him off the ropes, threw him to one side. He sat down hard, glared up at me, and appeared to be foaming at the mouth. And I thought: Oh, great . . . now I've got rabies. Crazy rolled to his feet and started a charge. I sidestepped, hit him a passing shot in the side of the head, then pursued and banged him into a corner. He crouched and covered and I ripped two uppercuts into his forearms. I stepped back to wipe the blood out of my eyes, and he leaped at me, head first, and hit me a head-butt that made me dizzy. I backed away, boxing. The jackass referee warned Crazy about butting accidentally, and that did it.

It took three of my best right hooks to set him up, but finally he was standing flat-footed, his back to the ropes, his massive upper arms working to keep his hands up. I moved in behind a left hook to the body, then went upstairs with a left-right, left-right barrage. He sagged, his hands down at his waist, his head snapping back and forth, and then, with a final right uppercut that had "sincerely starched" all over it, I drove him through the ropes and out onto the apron.

A silence hit the crowd for a moment, then it went into uproar. I walked back to the corner. Wash was beaming.

"Jeez cry, boy. You got a devil in you!"

"Yeah, well, the devil could use a few stitches."

The hotel lobby looked like a hospital room, so I felt right at home. Dr. Foote, a local practitioner with a clipped beard and a sonorous drawl, was taking selective stitches in nose, lips, and over one eye. Ace and Coop were standing by.

"Coop?" I said. "That guy's psychotic."

"Hold still, son," said Dr. Foote. "No eyebrow raising. Of course he's psychotic or he wouldn't be boxing."

"You call that boxing?" I said.

"I didn't see it, son. But he did a workmanlike job."

"He's going to get himself killed," Coop said.

"Sure," said Dr. Foote, "if he's lucky. Otherwise he'll be walking around on his heels with his mouth open catching flies."

"Doc," I said, "You don't understand. This guy is truly out of his mind."

"Oh, is he? And what does that make you?"

"Well, I'm not crazy."

"Really? Then why am I sitting here sewing you up?"

Coop and I went for a run the next morning, mostly along the top of the levee. Coop was in a good mood. He'd had a good fight, with a fast, accomplished man. He just wasn't in Coop's league, and Coop had put him down. Now he was shadowboxing, cavorting, enjoying himself. So I insisted on ruining his good mood.

"Coop? You don't think Crazy is crazy?

"Naw. He's what you call desperate. He don't like where he's at."

"Where he's at. You mean here?"

"No. Where he's really at. Somewhere south of Hind Tit."

"I don't get it."

"'Course you don't."

"Where's Hind Tit?"

"Nowhere. Or anywhere."

"Oh."

"See, like any black man, he wants out. So he's trying, using what he's got."

"He ain't got much."

"He don't know that." A heavy sigh. "He ain't got a chance. Oh, he go on fightin' his way north, playing the fool, until one day he gets lucky, and the white man asks him to visit. And he come walking up to this country store, and there's a white man on the porch, and he look at Crazy, and he say, "Welcome to Hind Tit, nigger. I own this place."

And Coop laughed, a hard laugh, as if he'd been there before.

"Now," I said, "I feel really bad about beating up on him."

"Oh, *sure*," Coop said. "*Now* he may *never* make it to Hind Tit!"

He laughed again, walked around in a circle.

"Coop? Are you angry with me?"

"Hell no, Catfish. I was just thinking that, if it makes you feel any better, the farther south we go, the more you be fightin' white boys."

"Why?"

"Because they don't like black boys fightin' white boys."

"Okay. Why not?"

"Well," Coop said. "If the black boy wins, he tends to get uppity."

"Can't blame him for that. So what if he gets uppity?"

"Why then they have to go to the trouble of cutting his balls off."

No laughter this time. No grin.

"They do that, Coop?"

"They do that, Cully. For laughs. Before breakfast."

"Jesus." I looked at him for a long moment. He was not in the least kidding.

"Thank God I beat him, then. Thank God."

"*Now* you got it straight," Coop said, somewhat coldly. And he turned and trotted off.

SEVEN

Let us go for a ride,
Don't you hear me crying.

Howlin' Wolf, "Smokestack Lightning"

It was about an hour down to New Madrid, and I told them all about the great New Madrid earthquake in 1811, the biggest earthquake ever to hit the North American continent. It was so powerful that it turned the Mississippi River around, so that it flows north here in a great hairpin turn all around the Missouri, Kentucky, and Tennessee borders for about seven miles.

"Bullshit," said Wash. "How the hell's it going to make the big river flow north?"

"Well, it cut across the channels, moved them apart, and created a big U-turn. That's a fact, Wash."

"You know what I think?"

"What?"

"I think you'd best stop readin' us from that damn book."

"Okay. Your loss."

"That's seventy-eight," Sonny said from the back seat.

The Tiny Grimes Quintet was doing "Midnight Special" on the radio, and I thought he was referring to the record speed.

"What's seventy-eight?" said Chappie.

"Them people out in that field," Sonny said. "Seventy-eight,"

Coop said, "He does that."

"He does what?" Wash said.

"Well," Coop said. "He looks at something, or a bunch of something, and tells you how many they is."

Wash said, "We went by that field at sixty-six miles an hour, and you counted seventy-eight people?"

"That's right," Sonny said.

"Shee-it," Wash said.

"No, wait a minute," I said. "There are people gifted like that. Incredible with numbers. They're called idiot savants."

"I go with the idiot part," Wash said.

I turned around to Sonny. "You been doing this all your life?"

"Yeah. When my Pap didn't beat me on the head."

"See, that's the trick," Wash said. "You get beat on the head enough, and you see things."

"Are you that good with numbers, Sonny?" I asked, delighted with the possibility.

"How much is twelve times two . . . no, twelve?" Chappie asked.

"Two hundred eighty-eight," Sonny said immediately.

"Wrong!" said Chappie. "It one hundred forty-four."

"Nope," I said. "You said twelve times two times twelve. That's two hundred—"

"Bullshit!" said Wash. "Only way we can check him is to go back and count."

"Why go back?" I said. "Here comes another field."

"Okay," Wash said. "Now we see."

Wash pulled over, and we all piled out. Lieutenant March pulled in behind us, as we all started counting.

"What do you say, Sonny?" I asked.

"One hundred three."

"Okay," I said. I counted as fast as I could. Then, "He's right."

Wash took a bit longer. Then said: "I'll be go to hell."

"Sixty-seven men and thirty-six women," Sonny said.

I counted the women. Thirty-six. I said, "Damn, Sonny, that's a great talent."

"What's going on?" asked March.

"Goddamn," Wash said, finishing his count. "He *is* a idiot."

"What did you say?" asked March.

"We got a genuine idiot with us," Wash said, and turned toward the car. "Could be very useful."

March stared after Wash, his mouth open. Was he being called an idiot? It was three days before I finally took mercy on him and explained about Sonny. As for Sonny, he was immediately put in charge of all restaurant checks and hotel bills, and he proved infallible.

New Madrid was not as prosperous as Cape Girardeau, and its hotel not as well maintained. Coop and I got a big, decaying room with twin beds and a view of the Dixie Theater. We met for lunch down in the threadbare dining room. The steak was first class but not so the service. No overt complaint about blacks, but a slightly strained atmosphere pervaded the dining room as the meal proceeded.

"Coop? You notice the waiters?"

"White," he said. "Don't like waitin' on black. That's why you got the biggest steak."

"Should I speak to them?"

"Hell, no. Then they poison us. Just relax. It gets worse, much worse, as we go south."

"Well, I'm not going to put up with it."

"Yes you are," Coop said. "Yes you are."

Wash dinged on a glass. "Got a announcement," he said. "Cully, you ain't fightin' tonight."

"Why not?"

"Take a look in the mirror."

"Hell, I've been cut up worse than this. By Coop."

"That was Chappie," Coop said.

"No way," Chappie said.

"Wash?" I said. "I can go."

"No, you cain't. I need you for Memphis."

"Can I know why?"

"The main man in Memphis," Wash said patiently, "is their middleweight. A white man, and former Tennessee state champion. So you be fightin' the main event against one tough dude." A pause. "Now, shut up and eat your steak."

I shut up.

The ring was set up in a lumberyard down by the levee. A storage shed, roofed and sideless, had been mostly cleared of lumber, with what remained used as bleacher seats. The ring looked tight, small, and brightly lit. It was a fine warm evening and I was luxuriating in the night off. I was in my best khaki uniform, and I tried to sit on the black side but was let known, in no uncertain terms, that I was not welcome. So I sat in the white section as close behind our corner as I could get, and was enlisted at once by Sergeant Kingdom to help with the stool, water bucket, and cuts. I was getting very good at cuts.

Coop was giving boxing lessons to a tall, rangy, somewhat older black man who looked very perturbed, it being clear that *he* was the one who usually did the instructing. Coop was enjoying himself immensely, showing off to the ladies at ringside, particularly to three black girls—all of them pretty, but one knock-down-drag-out beautiful—keeping his man in the near corner of the ring so as not to miss one yelp or squeal. He clinched in the corner, looking over the opponent's shoulder at the girls, holding the clinch just a beat or two too long for Wash to endure.

"Never mind the damn ladies!" he growled, and Coop backed away, threw a double combination so fast I could hardly see it, and down went the opponent. Coop bowed sweepingly to the ladies, and the fight was over.

All the rest of the team had pretty good bouts, and we came out of the evening five and two, which was acceptable to Wash.

I went to bed early, having left Coop at the door of a place called Hap's Bar, where he said the ladies had repaired. It was a rich, dark Missouri night, with the river lapping gently at the levee, and I went to bed with a fine feeling of well-being, of healing—in God's hands for sure.

I woke up suddenly, hearing noises like snuffling and choking, like someone in mortal *extremis*. I looked around from my bed (earlier in the evening, it had been shoved over against the far inner wall) toward the dim light from the window. After a couple of seconds, I could make out Coop, kneeling up in his bed, apparently suffering some kind of seizure. He gave out a little yelp, and I leaped from my bed and crossed to him just as he issued a profound groan and fell to his face.

"Coop! Coop! Good God, what is it?"

And then I saw the girl.

She screamed and Coop jumped out of the bed, saying, "Oh shit, man!"

"I thought you had a stomach cramp!"

The girl shrilled, "You told me he was deef and blind!"

I didn't know what the hell to do. The girl had pulled the top sheet up over her and was staring shock-eyed at me. And Coop was standing there shaking his head from side to side and making noises that sounded like violence just narrowly restrained.

I made for the door, stepped into the hallway, pulled the door shut behind me. And stood there in my olive drab shorts feeling very olive drab.

From inside came shrieks from the girl that must have been heard out on Cat Island, Louisiana.

"You son-of-a-bitch!"

"He used to be blind!"

"You goddamned liar!"

"It's a miracle, I tell you!"

"Right! Jesus Christ visited him while we were screwing!"

"I don't know what to say."

"You don't say anythin', you creep-ass! And that will cost you ten dollars!"

"Ten? That's double!"

"Shut up, or I'll make it twenty!"

I could hear some mumbling, then the sound of high heels spiking across the board floor toward the door. I looked around wildly, saw a small door across the corridor, and jumped at it. A broom closet. I put my foot into a bucket, pushed in against the broom and mop handles, and managed to get the door almost shut.

The door to the bedroom was snatched open, and here she came, the beautiful girl from the boxing match. Coop was right behind her.

"Let me walk you home," Coop said.

"You stay away from me! You shithead!"

And down the stairs she went, her heels striking like little hammers on the bare board steps.

Then other doors began to open.

Chappie said: "What the hell's happenin'?"

Then Waldo stuck his head out.

"Pecker Cooper strikes again!"

Then Wash came out of his room stark naked, blinking the light. "What the fuck you do, Cooper?"

"Nothin' I did." Coop said. "See, Madden, he had to come over and take a look."

Wash blinked at him. "Madden, huh? Well, whatever. Now let's cut this shit out and get some sleep."

Wash turned and went back into his room. The other doors closed. Coop looked around. "Cully?"

I eased out of the closet, the bucket still on one foot. I felt betrayed. "Why'd you have to tell him that? I thought you were dying."

Coop just looked at me for a moment. "Cully, you owe me ten bucks."

And he turned and went into our room. I stood there with my foot in the bucket for a time, then freed myself, and went back to bed. I lay there thinking that sometimes God's sense of humor was just too goddamned antic for words.

EIGHT

All you pretty women,
Stand in line.
I'll make love to you, baby,
In an hour's time.
I'm a man, I'm a man,
Oh yeah, oh yeah.

Muddy Waters, "Mannish Boy"

The next day was a holy day of obligation. I forget which one, but I think it had to do with the Blessed Virgin. I consulted with Wash, and he said as long as I was back right before lunch, he'd wait for me.

The New Madrid Catholic Church was very nearly full when I got there. The faithful had filled the parking lot. I even noticed a Greyhound bus parked at one end.

I knelt near the back and considered my sins. I concluded that nothing I had intentionally done would preclude my going to communion. And I was feeling a little in need of communion.

So I was examining my conscience when she arrived.

She was a quite beautiful, ash-blonde young lady, about seventeen, impeccably groomed and dressed, wearing a white suit, a broad-brimmed white straw hat trimmed with a red ribbon, white gloves, and white low-heeled shoes. She was carrying a small prayer book or missal covered in red leather and a matching red purse. She started up the aisle, saw that the church was all but full, turned, came back, genuflected next to my pew, and entered. Or tried to.

I was staring, transfixed. I had never seen a more beautiful creature in my life. I was frozen in place. She looked at me with some expectation, then softly (and ineffably sweetly!) said, "Excuse me?"

For a full five (or fifty-five, how the hell do I know) seconds, I couldn't move. And she was turning to go elsewhere when I finally made a spasmodic jump—and fell off the kneeler.

I struggled up, taking the kneeler with me. When I did manage to stand, the kneeler fell away from my shinbones and hit the floor with a sound like a magnum pistol shot. People stirred and looked around as I fell away to my left to make room, kicked the kneeler up again, fell back in the pew, driving both toes into the bottom of the pew in front of me. The kneeler came down again with a final bang, and I sat there, being shushed by the spectators and feeling like the biggest damned red-faced klutz in southern Missouri.

She entered the pew then, knelt down, blessed herself, and bowed her head, leaning her lovely face into her gloved hands, closing her eyes, and charitably shutting me out of her life forever.

I was poleaxed. I got to my knees again without disaster, and observed her in little glances. My God, she was gorgeous! I remember thinking: Beatrice, Rowena, Juliet, Cressida, and even Saint Therese the Little Flower! Isolde, and I her numbnuts Tristan! I was mortified, but desperately in love, and damned near missed communion. The lines were running down at the alter when I came to my senses. I glanced at her. Is this living saint not going to take communion? Apparently not. Dare I disturb her sweet prayer? Well, it was the only way I was going to get to the altar rail.

"Pardon me," I said.

"Of course," she said. She stood up, stepped out into the aisle, waited for me to exit. For a moment I couldn't move. She was smiling, and she might as well have hit me with a ball bat. I stood paralyzed.

Then, from behind me, "Go ahead, son. I'll keep an eye on her for you."

Giggles all around. I made the plunge, went clumping up to the altar rail, my face hot with embarrassment. I kept my eyes down as I returned to the pew. She rose, let me enter. I fell to my knees and put my red face in my hands. I didn't look at her, but was intensely aware of her presence, her barely perceptible perfume. In sliding past her, I had touched her, and my body was aflame at the least point of contact. Dear God, I thought. I am doomed. I will never make a priest. I have been seared at the soul.

The priest declared the mass at an end and the congregation began to file out. Suddenly she was on her feet and out in the aisle, and I clambered up and followed. She walked, radiant, out into the morning sun and headed straight for the diner. I will not fail to follow, I was telling myself. I will not fail to make contact.

I was right behind her when she entered the diner and was greeted by the hostess. "You alone, dearie?"

"Well, yes."

"It'll be a few minutes."

"I'm not really sure I have a few minutes. I'm with the bus."

"Excuse me," I managed to say. "If it would help, I'd be glad to—"

"I can put two in that half-booth."

"Well," she said, looking at me with a devastating eye. "If you don't mind."

"Two? Okay. This way."

"Thank you," she said to me.

"Oh, my God, don't mention . . . I mean, my privilege . . . pleasure."

I followed her to the narrow, two-person booth. On the radio behind the counter was Professor Longhair and his New Orleans Boys doing "Hey, Little Girl," with the professor on the vocal, which I had first heard a couple of days ago on the road. I took it as an omen of predestination. *This* was what God wanted for me.

As I sat down opposite her, she put her prayer book aside, removed her gloves, put them with her purse, just so, keeping her eyes down. There was a mirror on the wall of the booth, and, for the first time that morning I became aware of my several wounds: my fat, stitched-up lip, my several patches of bandage, one of them with oozed dry blood prominent on my right cheekbone. I immediately put up both hands to cover, and thanked God she wasn't looking at me.

"Coffee?" the waitress asked.

"Yes, please," she said.

"Sir?"

"Oh no, no," I said, reaching for my cup and turning it upside down with a clattering firmness that cut a big chip out of the saucer.

"Sorry, sorry," I said.

"What will you have to drink?"

"Milk, milk. I drink a lot of milk."

"I'm sure you do," said the waitress. Then, "You're on the bus, dearie, you'd best order now."

"Toast," she said. "Crisp white toast with butter."

"And you?"

"Oh, I—I'll have the same. Crisp."

The waitress moved away and as my eye followed her, I saw an awful sight. In a booth over against the far wall were Coop,

Chappie, Wash, and Spider. Coop was beaming at me, and Wash was holding up a forefinger-to-thumb greeting in front of a huge smile.

"Oh, God," I said involuntarily.

"Is something wrong?" she said, following my gaze.

"No, no, just some friends of mine."

"The coloreds?"

"Yes."

"Oh."

"We're a boxing team—traveling south."

"Boxing? Is that what happened to your face?"

"Yes," I said, covering it with both hands again.

"Well. It's nice that you took the time to go to church."

"Yeah, well."

The waitress put down our order. "Eat up, dearie. They're boarding already."

"Oh, dear."

The waitress put down two checks, and I pounced on them rather deftly, putting them under my toast.

"You don't have to do that."

"Yes I do," I said. "I make a lot of money."

"In the Army?"

"You'd be surprised, the way they pay their boxers."

"Thank you, then. But I'm afraid I have to run."

"Do you . . . do you, I mean, where are you going?"

"To New Orleans. I go to school there." She glanced toward the door. "Oh, there goes the driver." She grabbed up her purse and gloves, got to her feet. "Thank you again for breakfast."

I got to my feet, banging the table, spilling my milk. "You're very welcome. Have a nice trip."

She half-turned, half-waved, and was gone out the door. I watched as she crossed to the bus, got aboard. The door closed at once behind her, the bus roared into motion, made a turn onto the main street, and went quickly out of sight.

I was utterly deflated. Close to despair. And I was still staring after the empty hole the bus had left when Coop sidled up beside me.

"Hey, man. That was real tall cotton."

"What?" I said.

"I mean, she was high white merchandise. First class."

"Oh, yeah."

"This your prayer book?" the waitress said.

I regarded her dumbly. It was *her* prayer book, of course. A last object to cling to. But I hesitated.

Coop casually reached out and took the book. "Oh yeah. He borrowed it from me." Coop smiled his dazzling smile. The waitress smiled back.

"And here's the checks," said the waitress.

Coop didn't grab them. I fumbled out the money, paid, left a nice tip, smiled at the waitress, and stood there in something like shock. Then I reached out and snatched the prayer book out of Coop's hand. "You lied," I said. "It's hers."

"I know that man. Did you want the waitress to keep it?"

"No, no. I've got to return it to her."

"Right. Now all we got to do is catch that bus."

NINE

Now I stand at my window,
wring my hands and moan.
All I know is the one I love
is gone.

Arthur Crudup, "My Baby Left Me"

The prayer book was *The Book of Common Prayer*, and neatly lettered inside the front cover was:

Miss Cornelia Ellsworth
Miss Chamberlin's Episcopal Seminary for Young Ladies
New Orleans, Louisiana

So there was no need to catch up with the bus, though there was some discussion of it.

Wash said, "We'd lose Lieutenant March in the first five minutes."

Coop said, "What if we see it stopped somewhere?"

Wash said, "Why then we stop and Cully gives her her book."

Sonny said, "We ain't goin' to see it. It's long gone."

I said, "Look, I'll go to her school in New Orleans, and hand it to her personally."

Coop said, “They might not let you in, Catfish. Ain’t a seminary sort of like a convent?”

“Maybe, but it’s Episcopal, not Roman Catholic.”

“What’s the difference?” Chappie asked.

“Well,” I said, “they’re Protestants.”

“Yeah, but they still got nuns,” Coop said.

“If she goin’ to be a nun,” said Chappie, “it’s a natural shame. I mean, that’s real quality. No offense, Cully.”

“Well, I mean,” Coop said. “With Cully goin’ to be a priest hisself, it don’t make no never mind what she become. Cully ain’t got no truck with her nohow. Right, Cully?”

I guess I blushed, and Wash said, “Don’t you let them get to you, boy. You ain’t no priest yet.”

I heaved a great sigh. “Damn it, I’ve got her property, through no fault of my own, and I mean to return it to her. That’s all there is to it.”

There was a silence for a moment in the back seat, then, “You ever heard of the United States mail?” Coop said.

“Of course, I have. But . . . there’s no complete address.”

“You could look it up in the telephone book.”

“I suppose I could,” I snapped angrily. “And I might! But it’s my damn problem, and I’ll solve it in my own damned way!”

Another short silence. Then Coop murmured, “Besides, you can’t get laid by mail.”

I turned on him. “You shut up! Don’t you say another damned word!”

He shut up. But I could hear suppressed laughter—even from Wash—as I sat there burning with embarrassment. I did want to see her again. Of course I did. And what that said about aspirations toward the priesthood, I wasn’t sure. But I was sure that my intentions were pure, and that the mission was holy.

Wash closed the discussion: "I take you right up to the front door of that seminary, and I wait for you. And I don't want to hear no more from the back seat, y'hear?"

And there, of course, on the radio had to be Robert Johnson singing: "I'm a steady rollin' man, I roll both night and day. But I haven't got no sweet woman, boys, to be rollin' this-a-way." And I could see Coop in the back seat, his grin as wide as the rear view mirror.

The Air Force on its way through the cottonfields of Arkansas, headed for Memphis. Bo Carter singing "Pigmeat Is What I Crave," and Chappie strumming along on his guitar. The sun was high, but the old sagging black barns tell us we're getting into the poor South, crossing the poverty line for sure.

"How far to Memphis?" Wash said.

I glanced down at the map. "About fifty-eight miles."

"Well, we comin' up on Osceola. Time for a bit of steak."

"They got steak in Arkansas?" Coop said.

"Hell," Chappie said, "I'll eat anythin'."

And coming in from the near distance was a sign that said EAT. "It's also got gas pumps," I said to Wash.

"They must have red meat," Wash said. "Let's give it a try."

We pulled in, Lieutenant March close behind us. March never approved of anyplace we chose to eat, so there was no consulting him.

Up on the porch were six rocking chairs, all full of men in overalls and, apparently, chewing tobacco. They regarded us balefully, and not one made a perceptible move while we climbed the steps to the diner. Not even when I said: "Both of the cars could use some gas, if you got time."

As we entered I could hear a radio blaring a baseball game. The Dodgers and Cardinals, both very much involved in the pennant drive. Wash smiled around at me. "Jackie," he said.

We filed in, crossed to the counter. A large man in a blood-stained white apron observed us with an impassive eye. He was wearing a name tag that said "Jute."

"Your name Jute?" I asked.

He didn't answer. Then he spat a wad at the floor, and said, "He'p y'all?"

March said, "Do you serve lunch?"

"Naw. Just eats."

"Got any red meat?" Wash said.

"I got flanks and hog jowls."

"And pork bellies," Waldo said, *sotto voce*.

"What'd he say?" Jute said.

"He said we'll all have flanks, rare," Wash said.

Jute nodded dubiously. Then, "Niggras out back."

"Oh, for God's sake," I said. "We're the Air Force boxing team."

"Don't make no never mind. Niggras out back."

Wash walked over, took a look through a broken window. "You got no roof out back."

"Yeah. Wind blowed it off."

"Well, goddamn. The place is empty. You expect us to sit out there in the hot sun?"

Jute hesitated. Then, "Be okay for today. But don't come lookin' to do it again."

"Wouldn't dream of it," Wash said.

We all took seats at the far end of the restaurant, all ordered flank steak rare, and all noticed the raw armpit smell of the place. Lieutenant March took a small table by himself, and I could see him holding a handkerchief to his nose.

We were no sooner seated than the six redneck rockers from the porch trooped in and sat down at the counter. One of them asked Jute to turn up the sound on the ballgame—which was fine with us.

". . . one hopper to right . . . and he beats it out," the announcer was saying. "Which brings up the second baseman, Robinson."

"Jackie's up," said Wash.

"Listen to that crowd," said the announcer, over a chorus of boos. "He ain't all that popular here in Saint Louis."

"Goddamn nigger," said one of the rednecks at the counter.

"Ruin the fuckin' game," said a second.

"And he's yella where he ain't black," said a third.

I looked across at Coop, who was looking at me. We both stiffened a little.

". . . comes the fast ball," said the announcer. "And he gets all of it! *Gone* to deep center, and out of here! The Dodgers tie it in the eighth!"

"Shit nigger luck," said a redneck. "He cain't *bat*!"

I could stand it no longer. I turned toward the counter and delivered a small broadside. "What do you think he hit it with . . . his front teeth? You pathetic, pig-faced, satchel-assed troglodyte!"

"Oh shit," said Wash.

The biggest redneck was the first one off his stool and I figured it was my responsibility to engage him. I had to push Wash aside to do it, but I managed it, and met him coming in.

"You little fart," he said.

I moved quickly to one side, in imitation of Coop's patented walkby, and caught him full on the nose. Blood spurted—a prodigious amount of blood—and he grabbed at his nose, turned toward me, and I hit him three body shots, then a heart shot, and down he went. By this time, the others had come off their stools and joined the fray. And soon wished they hadn't. I saw Waldo hit one in the throat. His false teeth ejected like a sandwich at an automat. I saw Chappie hit another in the stomach: he issued a mighty wheeze, and suspired under a table. And I saw Coop tattoo a third, who just stood there, wild-eyed, going bloody at the face until Coop—mercifully, I thought—tagged him on the point of the chin and put him to sleep.

There were Air Force casualties, especially among the lighter weights. Mose got knocked flying through a screen-door, and Stone got thrown over the counter (he rose, coolly, and helped himself to a beer).

Wash performed in an outstanding manner. Shortly after the fight began—when I was helping Spider throw one of the rednecks out onto the porch—I saw Wash reach over the grocery counter, find a large paper bag, and proceed to take the steaks from all of the plates, and bag them. He then added a couple of loaves of bread, some candy bars, and probably a dozen Cokes and Nehis from the ice chest. He then took a coin from his pocket—a nickel or a quarter—put it on the counter, turned, and bellowed: "Boots and saddles, goddamn it! We're pulling out!"

The fighting was pretty well over. Two rednecks were still standing, but more or less falling back, so we retreated toward the cars. Lieutenant March was already in his car, waiting for us. The king of the noncombatants.

A little later we were well on down the road, happily eating steak sandwiches.

"Any cops, Cully?"

"Don't see any."

Sonny said, "Did you pay, coach?"

"No," Wash said, "he never presented me with a bill. But I left a nice tip."

Wash erupted in his joyous, barrel-roll laugh, reached over and turned on the radio. And it was Howlin' Wolf singing "Spoonful."

TEN

Mister Crump don't 'low
no easy riders here . . .
We don't care what Mister Crump don't 'low,
We gonna bar'l-house anyhow
Mister Crump don't 'low
no easy riders here.

W. C. Handy, "Memphis Blues"

It seemed that when we arrived in Memphis, we were almost immediately on Beale Street. And as we moved along it, Wash became almost reverent.

"You see there?" he said, pointing. "That there shotgun house? Well, that there's W. C. Handy's house. He wrote the "Saint Louis Blues" right there, by that front window.

"And there's the Old Daisy, and there's the New Daisy where we goin' to fight tonight. And right there is Mr. Handy's Blues Hall.

Chappie said, "We goin' to get to see any of this here? Hear us some music?"

Wash said, "You fight good tonight—real good—I take you out truckin' after."

A general cheer, and from somebody's loudspeaker we could hear Muddy Waters singing "I'm Your Hoochie Coochie Man."

We checked into a hotel, had a long nap, and got to the New Daisy early and got the taping done right. Wash seemed nervous. There was an undertone to Memphis that nobody had yet defined, but I could feel it, and I could tell it was pushing at Wash. It defined itself clearly a few hours later.

It was a raucous crowd even before the fighting started. We found ourselves in an old burlesque house with the ring down in front of the orchestra pit (which itself was full of tiered bleacher seats) and the stage lined with wooden folding chairs. The theater proper and the balcony were sold out, and when I came out of the ratty dressing room to have a look, the place was rocking.

Spider and Stone fought first and won, both on points. Then Chappie fought a huge young man who simply would not fall. Chappie said, "I hit him with everythin' I got, square on, and he wouldn't go. Son-of-a-bitch is made of stone." Waldo fought a draw with a real pro, a ringer and no question, and Mose knocked out a young man who was apparently afraid to get his hairdo mussed. Coop demolished a slow-moving target in the semi-main (Sonny had the mop up), and I was on against Mr. Percy Harpe, the only white man on the Memphis team, former Tennessee middleweight champion. He was renowned for his shotput right hand and his rock gut, but he had taken his share of punches in his time, which was about thirty-three years. Looking across the ring at him, I figured I'd add to his incoming punch total for a time before I tried to take him out.

He came on like a bullfighter, backing away from my jabs, inviting me to come in, whereupon he would move to one side or the other, throw one or two hooks, cover, and then back off again. I was astonished. I thought he was a pounder, a Dempsey, but he was almost a cutey.

In the corner after the first round, Wash said: "He settin' you up, Cully. He going to wait until you get careless, bring that right hand out of drag, and put you away."

"The hell he is," I said. "I got his right hand on radar."

"Keep it there. He hits like a piston. Remember that."

I remembered, but I didn't really believe it. So, near the end of the second round, when he did his usual fade away as I came on, I got a little careless, and turned to swing one as I went by. His right hand came out like a snake, hit me full in the mouth, and down I went. I sat there for a couple of counts, thinking: This bastard can really hit. Who taught him to cover and hide like that?

I got up as the bell rang. In the corner, Wash said: "You got to cover on the go-by! Goddamn, Cully, you ain't listening to me!"

And, just here, Ace Kingdom jumped in with a rare contradiction. "No, no. Make like you're goin' to clinch! Bump him hard! Then climb his near side!"

I wasn't sure what Ace meant, but he sure as hell meant it. I went out for the third tentatively, but old Harpe played right into my heavy hands. He came out (as I thought he would do all along) in a great rush, bulled right into me. I did exactly what Ace had told me to do. I pretended to clinch and hold. Harpe looked confused, muttered something, and, pushing me back with his left, uncorked an ill-advised, sweeping right. I moved inside it, brought the right uppercut, and deposited him on his hunkers. He jumped up blur-eyed, and I gave him the overhand right. This time he went down and stayed, his mouth open, heaving like a beached sea lion.

I had barely hit the stool when the referee, overseeing Harpe's seconds hauling him up off the canvas, grabbed Harpe's wrist and held his hand up, beckoned to me, and announced that the fight was a draw!

"Bullshit!" Wash howled. "You shitheels!"

Ace grinned at me quietly. "You done good, Cully. He killed a man two months ago in Nashville."

"Fine damned time to tell me," I said.

"That," Wash said, "was a first-class sincerely starched punch!" And they holdin' up *his* hand. Shee-it! They holdin' up everything but his pecker!"

And then it was the Air Force out on the town. I couldn't believe that I'd gotten out of my fight with an intact upper lip, but I had. And nobody else had gotten excessively damaged, so there we were, out on Beale Street, in our class A uniforms, looking like some of God's handsomest children.

I forget what night of the week it was, but Beale Street gave us its best. The joints and the honky-tonks were going full bore, street hawkers were in strident voice, pimps were openly soliciting custom, and whores in incredibly tight and brief sheaths were walking saucy little prance steps all over the sidewalk. There were dudes in black suits and brown derby hats just out there "looking sharp" and standing in line in front of Mr. Handy's Blues Hall, so many of them that we passed by—the place was obviously sold out. But we could hear Big Bill Broonzy, or a good imitation of him, singing "Spreadin' Snakes Blues."

When we got to Mitchell's Domino Lounge—one of the showplaces of the "Orange Mound" and featuring "The Brown Skin Models"—Wash held up one hand for a halt and went over to speak to the barkers at the door. I saw a little money passed and then Wash turned and waved the Air Force inside.

We got great seats down front on the right of the stage. The show was pure Memphis, with some originals and some fine imitations—Memphis Minnee, John Lee Hooker, Elmore James, Blind Boy Fuller, and, of course, the Brown Skin Models.

A male tap dancer came out and did such a virtuoso performance that he had the Air Force up and cheering throughout his last three minutes. He bowed to us repeatedly, and we knew we'd made the proper impression.

A buxom, vampish torch singer came out and sang—I forget what the hell it was, but it made no essential difference: we loved her, and she played to us until Coop and Waldo almost fell out of our boxes onto the stage.

A one-man band—complete with harmonicas, tap drums, steam whistles, and cymbals—did "The Stars and Stripes Forever" with such verve and feeling that he virtually brought the house down. He came back for an encore but got entangled in his equipment and fell down. He sort of crawled off the stage to great and sustained applause.

Then came the Brown Skin Models, and, as they said on their posters out front, "If You Ain't Seen 'em, You Ain't Seen Nothin'!" They were uniformly beautiful, turned out in nearly nothing, and I had a little trouble watching them at all. Some were a bit porky but all were full of bosom, verve, and black-stockinged sexuality, emphasized by flashing high heels. I frankly didn't think such a display was legal, but Coop, Waldo, Spider—and even Wash—had no trouble with any of it. And in fact Coop—who at one point had turned to me and said, "Great God, reverend, this is too goddamned much!"—vaulted over the rail of our box onto the stage and kissed one of the beauties. The beauty kissed back for a moment, then pushed Coop away, and he climbed back into the box with a beatific grin on his handsome face. It all ended in a grand finale, with bouncers lined up in front of the Air Force box to prevent further incursions and with Coop's particular Brown Skin Model throwing him kisses and, finally, a piece of her scanty apparel. Coop pressed it to his lips, and I knew I'd be in for a long night.

I was saying my night prayers when I heard the rattle of a key in the door. I jumped into bed, pulled the sheet up over my head, and froze. I could hear whispers and giggles, and then Coop saying quietly: "Don't worry. He sleeps like a dead cat."

After a moment, I fingered a fold in the top sheet, and took a look. In the light from the window (and a neon sign flashing rhythmically behind it) Coop was standing behind her, helping with something, kissing her on the shoulders. Her brassiere came off just as she reached down and brushed her panties away to the floor. She stood there revealed in all her splendor, and I damned near fainted. In fact, I couldn't look. I closed my eyes and reminded myself of hell fire, the angry God, and Christ on the cross. But I recovered enough to take another look—and they were gone, down on the bed, and groaning softly. Then the noises began to mount—lubricious noises, joyously animal. I covered my ears and said a "Hail Holy Queen," and, somewhere early on, being very, very tired, fell asleep.

I was shaken awake sometime later. By Coop, sitting on the edge of my bed, grinning wickedly.

"Hey, man," he said, "she like *you*."

"Oh my God," I said. "Have you no sense of propriety?" The girl, seated on the edge of Coop's bed, burst into giggles, and Coop sat there shaking his head and grinning. I pulled the sheet over my head, rolled to the wall, and stayed there.

At breakfast Wash had a small announcement. It was raining, and the chalkboard outside had rivulets running through its "Flapjacks, hogback, country eggs, grits" message. I was feeling down, very down, and not a little ridiculous. Coop simply had no concept of the value of virginity, and why the hell should he? Why the hell should anybody? Except, of course, for a Christian numbnuts who thinks he just might make a priest.

Wash, as usual, looked like he was about to announce the end of the world.

"Okay, shut up, while I talk at you. First, I want to congratulate you all on last night. We took 'em down good and proper. Except Sonny, who got robbed. They're a good tough team. And I know y'all's lookin' for a rest till we fight in Vicksburg tomorrow night. But . . . well, we got us a offer. To fight again tonight, here in Memphis."

I joined the general groan. We had done Memphis, and we'd done it fair and square, and I wanted no further part of it. Or, truth be told, no further part of Mr. Percy Harpe.

"I know, I know," Wash said, "you want out of here. And I will accept a no vote." He looked around, nodded firmly. "But hear me out. It's a lot of money—five hundred dollars, enough so I can offer each and ever' one of you twenty-five dollars, even if you don't fight tonight."

Well now he was talking. We listened.

"Okay. Here's the skinny. They only want three of us—Coop, Chappie, and Cully, especially Cully—and it's goin' to be a private fight, they say, with guards and such to keep it strictly legal."

This worried me.

"Who's sponsoring this, Wash?"

"I don't know. Some politician, what I hear. He don't like the way we dusted his boys, and he wants a return 'gagement."

"Who do I get?" I said.

"Percy Harpe." Wash said. He shrugged. "Piece of goddamned cake."

Right, I thought. Hardtack with a candle on it.

It was still raining that night, and I had a small case of the trots, and the last thing in the damned world I wanted to do was to climb in again against Percy Harpe. But we were a team, and twenty-five dollars was a lot of money, and I could do it, so I would.

They sent a black Cadillac limousine for us. There were actually three limos, one ahead of us and the other behind us, and we rolled in stately order down to the Chickasaw Bluffs, overlooking the dark Mississippi, and to a large brick factory building, painted white, looming in the night like a Foreign Legion fort. We pulled into a brick-paved archway and a courtyard beyond. Wash seemed very nervous but was containing it. I leaned over to him: "Is it okay, Wash?"

"It damn well better be," he said. I found out later that he had gone down to the Peabody Hotel, where, believe it or not, Lieutenant March had chosen to stay, and borrowed March's forty-five pistol. And he had it in his medical ditty bag as insurance against the five hundred being paid on time and in full.

"Who are these people?" I asked.

"Town's run by a man name of Crump," he said. "He's big on black Caddies."

"You seem concerned."

"I am. But just hang loose, and we be out of here in a hour."

The entry hall looked like a hospital, except for six black-hatted hardcases, real tough-looking torpedoes, flanking us as we entered. "You gentlemen work for a funeral parlor?" Wash asked as we went by. No answer.

"Cheer up," I said. "We'll be out of here in no time. Just as soon as we beat hell out of your people."

Still no answer. Wash eased forward. "Save it for the ring, Cully."

-81-

We were shown onto an elevator. One of the black hats spoke to Wash. "You brung the whole team."

"'Cept the lieutenant. He don't go out nights."

"We was only expectin' three."

"Well, this is the Air Force. We travel in squadrons."

"Dressin' room's on the third floor. The ring's on the second."

"Good," Wash said. "I want to see the ring. Soon's we get done with the wrappin'."

"Our boys are already wrapped."

"Well then, we got some unwrappin' to do."

"No, sir."

"Yes, sir. And any more from you, and we're headin' out that door. You got that? For sure?"

The black hat said nothing, the elevator doors closed, and we were committed, more or less.

Coop said, "Wash, I don't like this."

"I don't either, but by God we need that money, and we are gettin' it. After all this goddamn trouble."

We got to the dressing room, which looked like more hospital. I don't know what they made there, but it was antiseptic.

The other manager, a sleazy-looking white man named Tank, came in to watch Wash do our taping.

"I already did my boys," he said.

"Then undid them," Wash said. "I gotta see what's in there."

"Well, I thought after last night, you'd be more trusting."

"Not even close," Wash said. "Go unwrap them. I'll be right over."

"Okay, tight ass," Tank said. And went out.

"I may have to deck him before the evenin's over," Wash said. "Just watch my back."

The crowd looked like a delegation from a mortician's union, mostly in black and straw hats, all men, about thirty in number, about fifty in average age.

Chappie was up first, with a 250-pound black man who looked cross-eyed. Chappie told me later that whenever he tagged him, his eyes would come back into focus. Chappie pounded his arms awhile, and whatever punch the man had disappeared in massive peekaboo. Chappie clinched, glanced over at Wash, and Wash gave him the nod. Chappie stepped back, zinged four straight right hands, and the bout was over. I was working the corner, and when Chappie came over, Wash was shaking his head: "Stylish. Real stylish."

"Goddamn," Chappie said. "What'd you want me to do, sit on him?"

"No, no. You done good. I'm just wonderin' what the hell we're doin' here, if that's all they got to offer."

Coop's fight wasn't much either. This red-headed white kid came prancing out swinging, but in control, hitting hell out of Coop's gloves. Coop looked bored, played patty-pat awhile, took a mini-vacation. He boxed and cuffed until Wash shouted, "Damn it, Cooper! Get serious!" Coop looked over at Wash, raised his eyebrows—at that moment the redhead tried a truly purposeful combination. Coop accepted it on his elbows, stepped away to his right and delivered a perfect left hook. The redhead spun like a top, and landed flat on his back. There was no need for a count.

Coop came back to the dressing room shaking his head. "I don't know what's going on, Cully. That guy wasn't half as tough as the one I had last night. Why the hell are they paying us money for this?"

Chappie was there getting dressed. "I don't think they give a damn about you and me," he said to Coop. "They just wanted to give old Harpe another shot at Cully."

"Well," I said, "He's going to get it."

In the corner Wash said, "He's got to go down. And stay down. You know that."

"Aw, come on, Wash. He's a tough man. Give me a break."

"No. Can't do it. We don't put him down, they'll squiggle on us, like last night. He got to be out cold."

"Well, hell," I said. "Why not? He will receive my very best attention."

As I moved to the center of the ring, one of the black hats shouted, "Hand him his fuckin' head, Harpe!"

And Coop, from the back of the room, shouted, "Starch him, Cully!"

Harpe came out swinging, throwing the right lead three times in a row. I covered. His right was coming in very heavy, much heavier than last night. He's got himself ready, I thought. He's concentrating. But by the end of the first round, I knew it was more than that.

"Wash," I said as Ace worked my bloody nose, "he's hitting a ton."

"I know, boy. He's got his gloves packed."

"What?"

"Plaster of paris, probably. They injected it after I watched the tapin'."

"Well damn, Wash. Can't we call them on it?"

"Up to you. We call 'em, there's goes the money."

"Yeah, but if he ever tags me with that, there goes my front teeth."

"Like I say, up to you, Cully."

I looked up at Wash. "Never mind the money," I said. "The son-of-a-bitch has it coming."

Ace grinned. "That's my boy," he said.

"Stick and move," Wash said, "till you get him just right."

I got him just right near the end of the second round. He was throwing rights that came in like small pillows full of wet concrete, and my arms were hurting bad from blocking. But then, backing out of a short clinch, and off balance, he tried an uppercut. I caught it on my elbow. He gave a little yelp and danced away, shaking his right hand. I'd been waiting for the moment. I had never thrown a better overhand right. He went back into the ropes, came forward like a shot out of a sling, and hit hard on his face.

Wash had tears in his eyes when I came to the corner. "Goddamn," he said. "You show me somethin' that time."

We asked them to take Harpe's gloves off, but they tried to act offended, and he was still unconscious when they carried him out.

I was with Wash when he cornered Tank in their dressing room.

"You owe me money," Wash said.

Tank shook his head. "Deal's off. Your boy had something in his gloves."

"My boy?" Wash said. Then, not hesitating, he took out a pocketknife, crossed to Harpe—who was crapped out on the rubbing table—took his right hand, cut the glove off, and there it was. Shards of now-drying plaster of paris permeating the gauze wrapping on Harpe's hand.

At this moment, in walked Chief Hat with the referee.

"Got to disqualify your boy," the referee said.

Wash raised Harpe's right hand. "Bullshit," he said. "Look here."

Chief Hat said, "No contest. Cajun standoff."

"You know what that white stuff is?" Wash said.

"What is it?"

"Plaster of paris, is what it is. You packed his gloves."

All of the other members of the team had now crowded into the dressing room. Coop looked at Harpe's hand and said, "Why you dirty bastards! They could've killed you, Cully!"

"Now hold on," said Chief Hat. "We callin' this one even."

Wash dropped Harpe's hand, reached into his ditty bag, and

came out with March's forty-five. He worked the slide, held it down at his side. "We callin' this one double or nothin', fat chops. Unless you got the balls to kill the entire Air Force boxing team. 'Cause that's what it's goin' to take." Three other hats had sidled into the room, and Wash moved to cover them with his eyes. "I figure I can get about four of you before you can get your pieces out. You feel lucky?"

I'd never seen Wash like this. Not even close. I shivered and thought: Dear God, he means it. He really means it.

"Now, you heard me. You payin' double. A thousand cash. Lay it out."

Chief Hat hesitated for a moment. Then he said, "Pay him."

One of the other hats stepped forward, counted out the thousand at one end of the rubbing table, just above Harpe's head. Wash picked up the money, pocketed it, waved us out with his free hand. Chief Hat just looked at him, never said a word.

When we got down to the limos, the three drivers were leaning against one of the cars, smoking. Wash, pistol still in hand, addressed one of them. "We goin' home."

"Well, I don't know about that. I don't take orders from you."

"You do now," Wash said, putting the pistol in his face.

We piled into the limo. Wash got in next to the driver, whose hands shook visibly all the way back to our hotel.

"Pack up, right now," Wash said. "Never mind showers. Be down here in six minutes."

And we were. We had to stop at the Peabody for Lieutenant March. Got him out of bed.

"Sergeant Washington," he said, "I demand an explanation!"

"Sir, pack up and come on. Or don't. But we got people with pistols after us, and you may end up spendin' the night in the Shelby County morgue. Do I make myself clear?"

March packed. We told him the whole story later, when Wash gave his pistol back. His mouth hung open for a good two hours.

Later, after we'd stopped for gas and March was back in the second car, I asked Wash the big stupid question: "Wash, would you have shot them?"

Wash smiled. "First one to make a move wouldn't have left me much choice. Now would he?"

"Dear God," I said, "for a thousand dollars?"

"No," Wash said. "For the good of my belly. And your belly. So it wouldn't be gnawin' on us." He glanced at me. "You only get one belly, boy. Treat it right."

ELEVEN

Every cross-tie, bayou, and bog,
Way down where the Southern cross' the Dog.

W. C. Handy, "Yellow Dog Blues"

We stayed that night in Tunica, Mississippi. In a low-down, hot-sheet, bedbug motel (as Wash described it) so bad that Lieutenant March slept in the second car. I didn't much like the place, but I was thrilled, finally, to be in the Delta.

On one of our last weekends at Scott Field, I'd gone into St. Louis, found a bookstore, and bought the Viking *Portable James Joyce*, edited by Harry Levin. And while I was at it (and on recommendation of the book clerk), I bought the Viking *Portable Faulkner*, edited by Malcolm Cowley. The one with the maps of Yoknapatawpha County on the inside front and back covers. I'd been reading the Faulkner when I could ever since we'd gone on the road.

So here I was in the land of Quentin Compson, Herman Basket, the Sutpens, the Snopes, Colonel Sartoris and Will Varner, Dilsey, Popeye, Temple Drake, and Joe Christmas. I was only beginning to appreciate what Faulkner had done—but, starting with our motel, there was one thing I knew he had gotten right: the poverty. It had a smell to it: the rot of river bottom and bayou and vast muck-bucket swamps and tidelands. Those smells, but something deeper. If despair has a certain stench to it, that was what pervaded the air. Tunica County was one of the poorest in the nation and, my God, did it show.

The motel clerk had said to me when we checked in: "We don't take coloreds as a rule. But things bein' the way they are . . ."

"Real white of you," I said. "And how are things?"

"Well, we just ekin' by. Nobody's got no money to spend on *mo*-tels."

"Well," I said, "from what I can see, you'd best make a stand pretty damn soon, or you'll be out of business entirely."

"You think you got to tell me that? You think I don't know how far down we is?"

"I'm sorry," I said, and I was. The poor man looked close to tears.

"Next five dollars I get ahead, I think I'm goin' to start buildin' me a coffin," he said. And he meant it, and went shuffling off into the back room with the tears running down his cheeks.

And I thought: Dear God! I hope this is as bad as it gets. I can't take it any worse.

I had intended to leave him a five-dollar tip for being so accommodating regarding "coloreds." But now I couldn't. The poor bastard might just use it to buy coffin lumber.

Within three hours, we were all out of bed and out in the hall, inspecting one another for bedbugs. They were first-class, industrial-size bedbugs, and they bit like they were built in a forceps factory.

When Wash came out, he looked at us and said, "Shee-it. You people never see bedbugs before?"

I looked at him. "You're kidding, right?"

He smiled. "Count on it." Then: "All right, can't stay here. Hit the cars in ten minutes."

We did it in less. Lieutenant March said he was glad we had come to our senses, but he insisted on driving so as to get himself as far removed from the bedbuggers as possible.

We ran on down the road through Clarksdale, which was shuttered tight (it was about one in the morning), and kept on running, not quite sure what to do. But by the time we were coming up on Cleveland, nearly everybody had announced they were hungry. There was one bar-and-grill sign in Cleveland.

"That's it," said Wash. "Give the signal."

I stuck my arm out the window and waved and pointed so that March would prepare himself to pull over (a considerable operation, according to the Car-Two regulars), and we eased in among some other cars. There was a loudspeaker blaring—Wash said it was Big Bill Broonzy—and we started inside.

"Hey," said Waldo. "They got cabins."

"And a vacancy sign," said Mose.

"Sergeant," said Lieutenant March, "I don't know if this—"

"And who the hell ever did. *Sir*!" Wash said.

We went inside. We found a long room with a bar at one end and a dining area at the other. In the middle was a bandstand with a live band playing blues. There were only three couples out on the floor, and for some damned reason I thought of Cornelia. But I slapped the thought down at once: I could never bring her to a place like this.

A lanky white man wearing a nameplate that read "Kutch"

came out from behind the bar to intercept us at the front door. He was also wearing a forty-quart cowboy hat, cowboy boots, tight jeans, and a skillet-sized belt buckle.

"He'p y'all?"

March happened to be closest to him. "We thought we might have a late supper."

"Sure thing," Kutch said. "But Niggras got to eat in the kitchen."

"Then we Niggras will just have a drink," I said.

"Niggras got to drink in the kitchen, too."

"Well," I said, trying to hold it in (after all, it had been a long night), "suppose we rent three or four of those cabins?"

"You can rent 'em, boy, but no Niggras allowed in them."

I looked around at Coop. "That's three," I said.

"Three what?" said March.

"Three times he's said Niggra," I said.

Kutch squared himself around, addressed himself to Coop. "You don't like that, nigger?"

Mr. Kutch departed the vertical, coming down fully six feet away and skidding out onto the dance floor. There was the second of shock, then the barstools, the bandstand, and even the dining area started to empty.

"Let's do it outside!" Wash shouted, thinking of collateral damage and expenses.

So Coop and I took the rearguard. March skipped into the men's room, and the Air Force managed a strategic withdrawal to the parking lot.

This was a truly well-rounded, top drawer, knock-down-drag-out, piss-in-the-corner brawl, involving Ace and Wash from the outset, with Coop—as striker of the first blow—controlling the hot center of things. In the middle of it, somebody dragged March out of the men's room and through the front door, and I could hear him shouting: "I'm not with them! I'm not with them!" That was the night I truly wrote him off. They kicked his ass.

As it turned out there was a small outdoor dining area, and the battle quickly moved thence, it being a supply base for chairs, tables, serving racks and dishes, glasses, and a marvelous stock of ketchup and mustard bottles. There was some attempt by the locals to do damage to the Air Force vehicles, but Wash and Ace defended nicely.

I finally got off to one side, having received a stunning slosh to the right ear which got the blood running, and had the opportunity to observe the engagement for a moment. The Air Force was definitely holding its own, but the locals were showing a remarkable amount of dash and verve. I saw Stone hit one man so hard that his glass eye popped out and Spider Webb tattooing a man twice his size, three times his weight. The man finally came to a standstill, rolled his eyes to heaven, and toppled over like a felled tree.

There were four or five women on the front steps screaming so loudly that, at first, I didn't hear the police sirens. Two sheriff's cars came wailing into the parking lot, and then a third, out of which the sheriff alighted and—though things had quieted down a bit—pulled his revolver and fired three shots into the air.

"All right now! Who's the Niggra in charge?"

After a moment, Wash walked over to him, sort of dragging his right hand, and I thought, for an instant, that he was going to deck him. Certainly, the sheriff looked apprehensive. But Wash spoke to him quietly, then the sheriff boomed: "All you Niggras are under arrest! And that includes you white Niggras!"

I'd never been in jail before, and it was daunting. The stench was incredible. Overflowing toilets, antiseptic overkill, heavy smell of sweat, heavier smell of human misery. I gagged at first but gradually got used to it. I was worried about March, who might turn state's evidence, but he had avoided arrest and had simply disappeared. And I was a little worried about Wash, who seemed terribly depressed by the arrest. I tried to cheer him up, and he just looked at me for a time, then said, "You never done any time, have you?"

"No."

"It don't ever get any easier. It takes your balls off."

"We'll be out in the morning, Wash. I promise."

"You can't promise nothin', Cully. That redneck takes us on trial, we could be here for a year."

"They've got to fix bail."

"No, they don't."

When the sheriff, whose name was Custer, came around to lock down for the night, I said, "We're entitled to one telephone call, sheriff."

"That's right. Switchboard open at eight-thutty. Now shut your face." He ran his nightstick along the bars, hit the light switch, plunging the place into darkness, and sang out:

"Night y'all! Keep them black peckers in your pants!"

There was a clanging of several doors, then silence.

I looked to Coop. "This is incredible," I said.

"This is Mississippi," he said.

"What are we goin' to do, Cully?" Waldo said.

"We'll call the mayor."

"Shee-it," said Ace. "He own the jail."

"Well, maybe Lieutenant March will help."

"No, no," Wash said. "The son-of-a-bitch is in Tupelo by now."

"Okay, okay. We'll call the nearest Air Force base. How's that?"

"That," said Wash, "will get us a squad of Air Police and a quick transfer to their stockade."

I thought for a moment. My mother had some political connections. When they owned a house down by Hyde Park on the Hudson, my mother's mother, Agnes K. Murphy Mulligan, had gotten to know Eleanor Roosevelt. They'd stayed in touch. And just before I'd left for the Air Force, my mother had said something about the Air Force Secretary appointee being "a goddamned idiot named Stuart something, whose father deeply offended Eleanor one night at a charity ball when he . . ." And so on. I did not know who the Secretary of the Air Force was, but I thought it was certainly worth a try. My father had always told me, "Go right for the top every time. If you can get it into the Supreme Court, get it there." I told Wash what I had in mind.

"The Secretary of the Air Force! Jesus Christ, Cully! We'll end up in Alcatraz!"

"Well, what have you got in mind?"

"I'm goin' to take our thousand and bribe the man."

"Ah hell, Wash. We worked hard for that money. Let me try Washington first."

He issued a long sigh. "Okay, Cully. You take your shot. *Then* I'll bribe the man."

⌊⌉⌊⌉⌊⌉

The next morning at eight-thirty the sheriff, having handcuffed me, pointed to the telephone on his desk and said, "One call. And no bullshit."

I placed a collect call person-to-person to the Secretary of the Air Force.

"Do you have his name?" said the operator.

"That's a security matter," I said. "But my name is Cully Mulligan Madden."

"Yes, sir." Then she repeated my name twice, fiddled around, and finally got the number. "I believe this is the Pentagon," she said.

"Wherever," I said airily.

The sheriff was looking on and listening, slightly bug-eyed. He had just ordered fingerprinting and formal booking—which hadn't been done last night—so all the guys were within earshot. I played it with all the suavity I could muster.

A male secretary answered the phone. Not an assistant secretary—just a secretary. He asked the operator to repeat my name. The operator turned it back to me.

"This is Cully Mulligan Madden, acting captain of the Air Force boxing team, calling from the sheriff's office in Cleveland, Mississippi. I am calling collect because we are under arrest and duress, and have been illegally incarcerated while acting in the line of duty."

"We'll accept the call," said the secretary.

"They'll accept the call," I announced. Then there was a click-off, but no dial tone. I assumed I had been put on hold while the operator worked out the person-to-person collect business. So I took full advantage. "Yes, Mr. Secretary," I said. "Have you been informed of our situation?"

I pretended to listen, nodding and smiling. The sheriff looked like he was about to expire. "Wait a minute," he said. "Wait a damn minute here. You didn't say nothin' about line of duty, and all."

"Excuse me, sir? Oh yes, my mother's fine. She sends her very best." I listened again. "You'd like to speak to the sheriff? Of course. His name is Jody Custer, and I must say he needs speaking to."

The sheriff had begun backing away, holding up one hand. "No, no! Don't get me involved!"

Then the secretary came on and said that the Secretary was in conference, but that he would be glad to return my call within the hour. "Of course," I said. "Operator, would you please handle the details? Thank you." She clicked off. Dial tone. "Why," I said, "I'd be glad to speak to the Attorney General. This, in fact, is more in his line."

"Now goddamn it," Custer shouted. "This has gone far enough!" Then he composed himself. "I mean, son, I'm sure this can be worked out to everybody's satisfaction."

I wasn't going to let him off just yet. "You're with the director of the FBI? He'd like to speak to the sheriff? Yes, sir. He's right here." I held the phone out to the sheriff, hoping he wouldn't hear the dial tone, but he leaped back as if I were offering him a viper.

"No, shit! No way! No charges! All charges dropped!"

I spoke into the phone. "Well, it appears, sir, that we have solved our little problem here, and thank you very much." I listened. "My father is just fine, and thank you for asking. I certainly will, sir. Goodbye, and thank the Secretary for me."

I hung up. The sheriff, three deputy sheriffs, and the entire boxing team were staring at me in something like awe, jaws sagging, eyes bulging. Then the sheriff said, "You didn't tell him I dropped all the charges."

"Oh, no problem," I said. "He understood perfectly. Now, if you would be so good as to remove these handcuffs we'll be on our way."

The sheriff fairly leaped forward to get the handcuffs off and by God we *were* on our way in less than ten minutes.

The only delay was in finding Lieutenant March.

There were two other motels (aside from Kutch's) in town, and we found him at the second. He said that when the sheriff had impounded our automobiles, he had decided we were in real trouble and figured he ought to stay clear until he could arrange bail. He was lying, of course: it was about ten in the morning then, and he hadn't tried to arrange anything. He asked how we'd gotten out, but I just shrugged and said the sheriff had a soft spot for the military. He said, "Well, I just hope you didn't make any representations that might reflect upon my record." We should have driven off and left him right then—I know Wash was ready—but mercy prevailed. Ace did tell him that from now on he, Ace, would do the driving. March said he was used to being chauffeured, and that was fine with him. People like March don't come along often, but when they do they are to be assiduously avoided.

We were a few miles down the road when Wash chuckled, looked over at me. "The Secretary of the Air Force was real cordial, was he?"

"Oh yeah," I said.

"Sent his best to your mother?"

"He did."

"And the director of the FBI sent *his* best to your father?"

"That's right," I said, wondering if I shouldn't admit to the whole fraud.

But Wash was shaking his head and laughing quietly. "Goddamn, Cully, forget bein' a priest. You got a great future ahead of you on Broadway."

So I'd apparently fooled everybody but Wash.

Later Wash told me that Cleveland, Mississippi, was supposed to be the birthplace of blues music. Judging by their jail, I'd say they have a pretty fair claim.

TWELVE

Oh Mississippi, oh Mississippi,
My heart cries out for you. . . .
I'm goin' to Tishomingo. . . .
Where they play the weary blues.

Spencer Williams, "Tishomingo Blues"

We stopped at Greenville to buy some itching powder for Waldo and Mose, who had made a lot of friends among the bedbugs, and to refill Ace's first-aid kit, which was running short of bandage, iodine, and witch hazel. Wash called ahead to Vicksburg to get our hotel's name, and came back to the car cursing and swinging his right fist in the air.

"Them sons-of-bitches! Pissants!"

"What's wrong?"

"They cancelin' on us! Them Vicksburg bastards!"

"How come?"

"They an all-white team, and they don't like to fight black boys!"

Wash punched the car a couple of times, and Ace said we ought to sue them, but I was secretly glad to get a night off. My right ear was still oozing blood, and my left arm had some kind of a kink in it. Lieutenant March came forward to offer his plan: We'd go down to Vicksburg, find a nice hotel, and hot baths and a decent dinner. Wash gave him a murderous look. "You willin' to foot the bill? *Sir?*" March wasn't.

Then Waldo said, "You know what? My mama's folks lives just south of here. Place called Island 92."

"Island 92?" Wash said. "Hell, I been there! Best stump whiskey in the Delta! And all them blues players come south out of Clarksdale! Shee-it! Saddle up!"

"I craves catfish!" Ace said.

"I don't much like catfish," March said.

"Then we gets you a bucket of hot tamales at Dixie Doe's!" Wash said. "Whoo-ee!"

The road to Island 92 wasn't much, and I kept wondering what the hell kept it from sinking quietly into the swamp. This was black Delta marsh country, built on whatever islands the river had left for building. And the town of Island 92 looked like the first strong wind would blow it into Yazoo City. There was a four-corners store, a black church, a shack bar, and a shotgun shack restaurant advertising crappie, bass, bream, and catfish in large letters. It looked like the ptomaine capital of the Southeast, and I was pleased that we had other plans.

Waldo came out of the restaurant grinning.

"Ain't but three, four mile out. Toward of Eudora."

"Well, then." Wash said. "Will they sell us some catfish in there? I mean, we can't just ten, eleven of us walk in on yo' people."

"Hell," Waldo said. "Them restaurant people wants to give us the catfish. I mean, they knows my Aunt May and Uncle Walter real well."

Wash climbed out of the car, reaching for his wallet. "Come on Waldo. Folks like that deserves to get paid, like it or not." Wash turned and beckoned to me, and I went in with him holding one hand on my shoulder. "We got to get you educated about how the real black folks live," he said.

The restaurant was early American long plank with bare tables and a counter where you picked up your food. There was a sign that announced the menu: all kinds of fish, collard greens, red gravy, and chitlins. In the back a huge man was working the stove, and an even bigger woman left off cleaning some fish and came to the counter window.

"Well," she said to Wash, "ain't *you* somethin', with yo' stripes and medals and all."

Wash grinned. "I ain't nothin', mama, but poor enlisted folk."

"What can I do for you, handsome?"

"Wanted some catfish, take out to Waldo's people."

"How's about a dozen?"

"Better make it two dozen."

"These are real fat fellers."

"My boys eat 'em two at a time."

"Well," she said, laughing. "His Aunt May fries 'em up fo' y'all, you got a feast comin'."

"Now I wants to pay."

(I noticed that Wash had slipped into the Delta patois, at least the drawl of it, but that was part of his immense charm.)

"No pay. And I got some nice grits and cornpone and some of the best chitlins you ever put a tooth on."

"All of it," Wash said, grinning. "But . . . we pays." And he put a twenty-dollar bill on the counter.

She looked at him, eyes glinting. "Matter of policy?"

"Matter of pride."

I think, by now, she was in love. "Damn, Sergeant," she said. "You got a way with you. You does indeed." Then she turned and called to the man at the stove. "Brother Finlay? Got a order for the works!"

Brother Finlay smiled a dazzling smile and got right down to business. Wash spoke softly to me. "I got to go over to the store and negotiate us somethin' to drink. I see you at the car."

As Wash went out, the large woman came rushing back to the counter window. "Where he goin'?"

"To buy us some soft drinks, I think."

"Soft drinks," she said, fairly purring. "And mebbe a little sour mash." She smiled at me sweetly. "You tell him my name's Lilah Meek, an' he ought to stop by again aroun' six."

"I'll tell him."

"An' what's *his* name?"

"Master Sergeant Washington."

"Yeah. Yeah. I bet he's a master."

When I got back to the car, Wash had just arrived with the soft drinks and a couple of jars of the hard. He got directions from Waldo, and we set out for Aunt May's with the aromas from the hot brown paper bags of food filling the car. I told Wash what Lilah Meek had said. He shook his head, gave his best wine-barrel chuckle. "Woman like that," he said, "she'd snap you off at the nub."

About a mile out, the road began to get truly meager. It was packed with potholes full of swamp water, and it turned from macadam to dirt and back again in the space of fifty yards.

"I smell snakes," Mose said.

"Jesus pistol Christ," Wash said. "These people got to live in a rowboat!"

We seemed to be getting deeper into a jungle full of catfish farms and magnolia and weeping willow and big oak trees, all being covered and choked by lush big-leafed kudzu. The road grew smaller, more serpentine, and took to coming to dead ends without notice. And we began to see snakes stretched out lazily on the pavement. Some of the time we passed right over them and they didn't move. We came to one place where the water covered the road. It descended into the swamp and came up about twenty feet later. There was no telling how deep the water was, so Wash eased into it slowly and pushed across. It never got more than a foot deep, but Wash said: "Goddamn, I hope it's high water right now or we're never goin' to get out of here."

"I just thought I saw something," I said.

"Like what?"

"It was sort of long and moldy green."

"Did it have its mouth open?"

"No, no. A building."

And then we saw it. The home of Walter and May Toller, Waldo Waldron's maternal aunt and uncle. The quintessential swamp shack barely afloat on a pond of mud. The closer we got, the more doubtful it became that there was room to park. We just made it, on about fifteen square feet of the last land before a wooden bridge crossed to the shack.

"How the hell we ever goin' to turn around?" Wash said.

"I wouldn't worry," said Coop. "Goddamn cars goin' to sink out of sight in about one hour."

Waldo leaped out and went running across the bridge and into the house without knocking. And we climbed out a little reluctantly, not at all sure we should have come.

"Sergeant Washington," Lieutenant March said, "this time I really must protest."

"Respect their house, sir," Wash said softly.

Then Aunt May and Uncle Walter came out of the house smiling and waving. We trooped single-file across the bridge to meet them, March bringing up the rear, and Wash made the introductions with style and grace. Uncle Walter had three top teeth that made up his smile, and one of them was gold. It gleamed in the sun benevolently, and I don't think he stopped smiling the whole time we were there. Aunt May was one of those people whom you love at first sight. In five minutes, we felt privileged to be there. Except, of course, for March, whose conduct caused me to begin planning to drown him unobtrusively before the day was out.

The shack was clean as an old bone, and about the same color inside. There were only two rooms—a tiny bedroom and the rest of it given over to kitchen. There was a big wood stove with skillets hanging over it, a large kitchen table with benches (they had raised eight children in that shack, and all, by the singular grace of God, had survived childhood and gone on to other places, other lives), and hanging on the wall was an old shotgun, about ten fishing poles, and an ancient, battered twelve-string guitar. There was a narrow deck that ran around most of the shack, with several doors leading out to it.

The catfish and the drinks were brought in, and Aunt May—who seemed to burble nonstop with sweet-natured, gentle laughter—had the stove fired up, the skillets laid out, and the fish skinned, dipped, and breaded in just no damn time at all. Wash, Ace, and Uncle Walter were sampling the sour mash, even Chappie got a sip, and, except for March, everybody was having a hell of a time.

When the smoke from the frying catfish got a little heavy, I went out onto the deck. Spider was there drinking a Nehi and staring out into the bayou. March was also there, staring down into a moored rowboat at a large water moccasin that was coiled fatly in the bow.

March looked at me and pointed at the snake. "Isn't anybody going to do anything?" he said.

"Yes," I said. "We have called the local authorities."

"They have a telephone?"

"No, sir. They use a small drum."

"I didn't hear anything."

"Well, sir," I said, "you have to have an ear for it. Very subtle."

He looked at me, nodded slightly, and I turned away, feeling a large grin coming on.

I went over to Spider, who was smiling covertly, shaking his head.

"Is they a bigger damn fool anywhere?" he said softly. "How the hell did he get to be a officer?"

"Well, they can always use a good idiot. To talk to congress. Things like that."

"Cully, you too damn much."

"Yeah. I got my sense of humor living with my mother. It was laugh or die time. All the time."

"Your parents still happy married?"

"No, they're divorced. Haven't I mentioned that?"

"You never said a word about your family."

"It's not a happy subject," I said. "But I'll inflict it on you one of these days."

"That's okay," he said. "Hang easy."

"Seen any new turtles?" I said, indicating the bayou.

"Nope. Lots of ghosts."

"Ghosts? You believe in ghosts?"

"Believe in them? Why, Cully, they all around us. Especially in a place like this."

"You're serious?"

"Absolutely." He looked at me closely, to see if I was believing him. "You got to believe in ghosts."

"Well, I'm open to persuasion."

"Okay. See, a black man's soul runs south when he dies, generally along the river. He got to find where his mother birthed him. Gave him suck."

"That makes sense."

"Sure. And this whole Delta is swarmin' with ghosts."

"Any particular reason?"

"Yeah. From what I'm hearin'."

"Hearing? Right now?"

"Yes, indeed." He paused for a moment, as if he were in fact listening. Then he said: "In April, 1864, Nathan Bedford Forrest, the Confederate general, sabred, him and his riders, about seven hundred black soldiers, their women, and their children at Fort Pillow. Across from Osceola."

"Christ."

"Lot of them around here, still headin' south."

"Still here?"

"Ghost time isn't like our time."

"Right."

"But the biggest bunch aren't from Fort Pillow."

He liked me to prompt him, so I did. "Where, then?"

"You ever hear of Elaine, Arkansas? Where the writer Richard Wright was born?"

"No. I don't think so."

"Very close to Helena. Well, in 1919, they was a three-day riot. The whites blamed the blacks, but it was the whites who did the killin'. Between four and five thousand black folks were murdered, *massacred* in Phillips County."

"Good God. This is true?"

"As God is my witness. They put one hundred and twenty some black men on trial. But not one white man was indicted."

"How come I never heard of it?"

"Oh, the Arkansas newspapers plowed it under. Let's see. That was twenty-eight years ago. That ain't so long, is it?"

"And their ghosts are still here? Right now?"

"An awful lot of them. Most were Southern born. I mean, deep South. And they are still lookin' south, most of their poor souls still passin' through here, and they are plum wore out with sorrow. They talkin' at me right now, and I'm tellin' them what I know."

"And what's that?"

"That there's a black heaven, where the black God makes the rules. I tell them they got to let go of this here to get to heaven. But they don't all listen too good."

"Aren't they afraid of me? A white man?"

"No, Cully. They ain't afraid of you. They know you got soul."

"Thank you, Tree."

Then came the call to come and get it, and we went in to eat.

⌐¬⌐¬⌐¬

It was one of the all-time great meals. Corn bread, grits, collard greens, fried tomatoes, and the catfish, cooked whole and slightly blackened with a hot sauce. There were a couple of pitchers of milk, and another couple of pitchers of some kind of homemade wine (maybe dandelion) that we were allowed to sample, and, of course, there was still an ample supply of sour mash. Wash was feeling expansive, and told us about his gym in New Iberia, Louisiana, which had been left to him by a former fighter, a white man, who had always thought that Wash should have been heavyweight champion. Wash said: "He was dreamin', of course. I never had the power to fight big-time."

"You never had the power?" I said, not believing it for a minute.

"Nope, nope, and nope," he said. "Look. Some people got it, some ain't. A heavy hand, a punch that takes people down. Coop got it, Chappie got some of it. And you, Cully, you got all of it, when you put your mind to it."

"I don't believe that," I said.

"You don't have to believe it. You got it from your daddy, and you get mad enough, it'll be there."

I could see I had annoyed him, so I let it go.

But was it true? I hadn't told anybody yet that my father had once fought an exhibition with Jack Dempsey at the

Canandaigua Outlet in upstate New York. I believe the date was July 4, 1917. And that my father and Dempsey had become friends. And that my father, on two occasions, had taken me to Jack Dempsey's restaurant in New York City, and both times, by prearrangement, Dempsey was waiting for us. And, finally, that the affection between the two men was obvious, and that Dempsey had once leaned to me and said, "Your father hit me once harder than any other man ever did." And that, another time, I distinctly remember Dempsey saying, "Ed, I should have done what you did. Become a lawyer. At least gotten an education." I hadn't told them any of these things, and I'm not sure what difference it would have made. Wash somehow knew that I had my father's right hand, and that's all he needed to know.

But then something happened that has to fall under the category of incredible. Wash was talking about the toughest fight he ever had, and I was listening closely, and he said, "His name was Cyclone Williams, and he was the toughest man, white or black, I ever got in the ring with. And, hell, he must have been thirty-five or forty at the time."

I was staring at him. "Did you say Cyclone Williams?"

"That's the man's name."

"Well, Wash, my God. My father fought a man named Cyclone Williams five times. In the Saint Nicholas arena in New York."

"Bite your tongue," Wash said.

"Unless there were two Cyclones."

"Ain't but one." He was looking at me, not quite believing me. "What's your daddy's name?"

"Edward Madden. He fought under the name of Indian Ed Madden for some reason. He looked a little like an Indian, I guess."

Now Wash was staring at me. "Goddamn," he said reverently. "No wonder you got a right hand. Your daddy was Indian Ed Madden? I saw your daddy fight once, in Trenton, New Jersey. Fought a man name of Flynn, I believe it was. Big, strappin' man. And your daddy sincerely starched him in the third round. My God!" Wash got to his feet, stomped on the wide-board floor, clapped his hands to his thighs, and then bent his face down close to mine. "Your daddy *beat* Cyclone Williams three times!"

"That's right. They drew one, and Cyclone won the last one on points."

"Damn, damn, damn," Wash said softly. "It's true. It's accurate." He looked around at the others, who were watching Wash big-eyed. "Excuse me, ladies and gentlemen. Don't let me interrupt your dinner. But I—I, I'd best have another drink."

And he did. But he kept glancing at me and shaking his head, and I finally told him about how I had met Cyclone Williams.

My father and I were walking across the Albany railroad station when we encountered a large black man pushing a broom across the marble floor. As we came on, he stopped, looked at my father.

"Counselor?" he said.

My father looked at him. "Cyclone?" he said.

They rushed into each other's arms, and I remember the dust rising from my father's overcoat as Cyclone beat on his back with his great, gnarly hands. My father insisted on buying a drink, so Cyclone leaned his broom against the wall, and we went to the station bar. I think I was five or six then, and I had sarsaparilla and sat there in awe, looking up at these two giants talking of ancient battles and remembering and loving each other. I've often thought that my feeling of kinship with black men—my deep sense of our common humanity—finds its roots in those moments. I also began to learn a disquieting, more complicated lesson about how love, heroism, and honor—which like gold should serve as common currency in any realm—in my homeland were esteemed less than brutality in a white man if the man whose wealth in virtue was black. How else could I understand the broom in Cyclone's hand and the briefcase in my father's? Two men who had fought and loved each other as equals in the ring had to live as beings alien to one another in the world outside it. I didn't tell Wash any of this. I didn't have to.

When dinner was over, Uncle Walter took the twelve-string guitar down from the wall and tuned it as we cleared the table, pushed back the chairs, and formed a half-circle around him. I have an indelible memory of Uncle Walter, seated on a straight chair next to the fireplace, delivering himself of one of the finest guitar and vocal concerts I've ever heard.

He started with "No More, My Lawd," "It Makes a Long Time Man Feel Bad," "Levee Camp Holler," "Penitentiary Blues," and "Stackerlee." Between the songs, there was silence. But when he paused and took a drink, there was wild, sustained applause. Even March—who had shut up about the snake getting into the house—clapped vigorously.

The second set was all Huddie Ledbetter, many of them prison songs. And the way Uncle Walter sang them, you knew he had been there and back, and you could hear the long anguish and humiliation of his life. Your heart broke to hear it.

And he sang "Take This Hammer," "The Eagle Rocks," "Rock Island Line," "Ella Speed," "Backwater Blues," "Take Me Baby," "Saint Mary Blues," and, to end triumphantly, "Midnight Special," done with such feeling and power that he left us, at the end, slapped flat. We just sat there for a moment, stunned, then broke into applause, hoots, shouts for more. But the old man was done. He smiled and bowed; the evening was over.

We said our goodbyes and went out to the cars happier than we'd ever been—renewed, full of fire, sour mash, and wine, ready to demolish marines and whomever. Wash, observing the spirit of the occasion, didn't worry about turning around. He simply put that Hudson in gear, charged off into the bayou. We did a mighty U-turn, throwing mud and slime, but came up on the road doing fifty miles an hour, with a rooster-tail of muck standing six feet in the air behind us. Ace managed to follow, at a respectful distance, and old Wash was laughing and wagging his head and saying that that was just maybe the best goddamned time he'd ever had.

THIRTEEN

It makes a long-time man feel bad,
It makes a long-time man feel bad,
my Lawdy, Lawdy,
When he can't-a-can't-a get a letter
My Lawdy, from home.

Alan Lomax, Negro prisoners singing,
Parchman, Miss., 1947

After a night at a reasonably clean motel, we went through Vicksburg too damned briskly, but Wash was angry at Vicksburg, and the statuary and battlegrounds had to be absorbed at the gallop. I felt good, if slightly hungover from the wine, and B. B. King was on the radio singing "The Thrill Is Gone." I thought the fight in Natchez would be a tonic for all of us, especially Mose, who had kept Chappie up all night "carryin' on."

"What was he carryin' on about?" I asked Chappie.

"Oh, all them prison songs."

"No damn wonder," said Coop. "With his daddy doin' life at Angola."

"He is?" I said. "For what?"

"Murder. What else."

"And no parole," said Chappie.

"Who'd he kill?"

"A white man," Chappie said. "He fired both barrels at Mose's father. But he missed. Mose's father hit the white man with a two by four while he was tryin' to reload." Chappie paused. Then, "Open and shut cast of unprovoked homicide."

"Mose sure love his daddy," Sonny said.

"He come around," said Wash. "That book say anythin' about the Natchez Trace?"

"It says it's got a thirty-five-mile-an-hour speed limit."

"So, stay on sixty-one?"

"Right."

"We runnin' a little tight. I mean, we got to find steak for lunch."

"Grand Gulf looks all right."

"What about Port Gibson?"

"Probably better."

"Yeah. That's a good old town."

Port Gibson had a diner that served a rump steak that had been pounded into submission, but it was edible. The owner had been in the Army in both World Wars and had no problem serving blacks as long as they were in uniform. But he was still a redneck and couldn't keep his mouth shut. He beckoned me over to the cash register, and said, "You gettin' extra pay for this?"

"For what?"

"Travelin' with them coloreds."

"I don't mind."

"You could get yourself killed anywhere south of here. Take my word."

"Thank you," I said, "but, see, I'm a quadroon myself."

He blinked at me. "Oh, shit, then," he said. "Oh shit for sure."

We got into Natchez late, in a driving rainstorm. I'd enjoyed the ride down, running through the piney woods with the smell of the wet trees heavy in the air. But the rain had gotten heavier and I could barely see the street signs.

"He said turn left at Nellie's?"

"That's what the man said."

"Well, I don't see it."

"You'd best see somethin' soon, boy, or we'll be in the river."

Then I saw Nellie's sign, which had partly fallen down but was well-lighted.

"Okay," Wash said. "Now we under-the-hill. Now we turn left."

The "site of the fight," as I liked to say, was an old ballpark. As we arrived, it suddenly stopped raining, and we could see that it wasn't much of a site. A clapboard grandstand that was coming apart, with the ring set up on the pitcher's mound. The ring posts had been pounded into the ground, and some attempt had been made to pack the earth in the ring proper. The spectators were mostly accommodated on planks across wooden beer crates, the whites on three sides, the blacks on the fourth, as usual. There were two floodlights that were barely adequate, especially since they kept blinking on and off.

A fat man whose name was Schute came growling up to us.

"Where the hell you been?"

"Oh," Wash said, "we stopped off at Nellie's to get laid."

"Very funny. Dressin' rooms under the grandstand. You got a feather, he's first up."

We piled out and started unloading our gear. Wash was looking at a fight card that Schute had given him.

"I heard of this feather," he said to Stone. "Fact I seen him fight once, over in Gretna. Hops around like a potful of gum-balls."

"So? What's the drill?" Stone said.

"Hit him between his gums and his balls."

There were a lot of spiders in the dressing room, contentious little bastards that seemed to think they owned the place.

Mose said they were banjos, which I didn't understand at the time, but when one bit me on the ankle and it hurt like hell and raised a bump, I decided they were to be shown some respect. We moved the dressing room out into the hallway.

I worked the corner with Wash and Ace for the first few fights. Stone pursued Gumballs relentlessly throughout the first round, but couldn't catch him.

"You ain't hit him once, full on," Wash said.

"How the hell can I? He don't light nowhere long enough to hit him."

Ace said: "He got big feet. Step on his toes."

Stone went out, let Gumballs hit him a couple of shots while he studied Gumballs's feet. Gumballs finally got brave, and stuck out his left foot as he prepared a conclusive right hand. Stone moved in, planted his left foot on Gumballs's left foot, and put a right hand on Gumballs's mouth that effectively ended his evening. Gumballs's manager came rushing out of his corner to protest, but slipped and fell face down in the mud.

And then the skies opened up, the lights shorted out, and the crowd began to howl and stomp. I went back to the dressing room with Stone and the place was shaking under the feet of the crowd.

Coop grinned at me. "Hey, maybe we get another night off?"

"Mose could sure use it," I said quietly, looking to where Mose was sitting, staring at the wall, as he had been doing since the night at Uncle Walter's.

"The closer we get to his daddy, the worse he is."

"I'm going to talk to Wash, maybe send him back."

Wash came in at that moment. "Hey, Coop, Cully, you got to fight a exhibition. Right now!"

"How come?" Coop said.

"They two boys afraid of lightning."

"Well, I'm not so goddamned fond of it myself," Coop said.

"Come on," Wash said. "It'll save the stake money."

"Well, we got to eat," Coop said.

A large part of the crowd was still there, and the rain had pretty well stopped. So Coop and I agreed to put on a good show, consistent with not hurting one another. But during the first clinch, Coop got giggling, slipped, and went down into the mud. I tried to help him up and he pulled me down with him. And we turned it into a mud wrestling match. The mud was thick, like black plaster, and I was covered head to toe. The crowd loved it, but Wash, who'd arrived late, was outraged.

"Goddamn it!" he roared. "Get up out of there! Make it a contest!"

"It *is* a contest," Coop said. "We get all done, you got to guess which one's the colored man."

We kept it up and we were the hit of the evening. And Wash got his stake money, which was all that mattered. I was voted blacker than Coop, which, by the end, I certainly was.

We checked into an old black hotel whose hot water was its only virtue. When I came of the shower, Coop was all turned out in his best class A uniform, newly ironed on a board he'd found in the closet.

"What's this?" I said.

"This is the prettiest one gentleman of military color you ever clap eyes on."

"But what's the occasion?"

"You remember Nellie's we passed on the way in?"

"Yeah."

"Well, Nellie's just happens to be the finest whorehouse in the South. Includin' New Orleans."

"You mean you're going to a whorehouse?"

"Shockin', ain't it? A stud like me spendin' good money on it. But it's a learnin' experience, Cully. Think of it that way."

"It's disgusting, is what it is," I said. "You degrade yourself, *and* the woman. You—"

"Cully, Cully," he said, putting tips of fingers to forehead as he ducked out the door. "You just think of me learnin'."

When he got home, I had just gotten to bed and he came over and sat down on my side. He heaved a sigh. "Cully," he said, "you are now roomin' with the smartest son-of-a-bitch in America."

FOURTEEN

I don't want no cold iron shackles
I don't want no cold iron shackles
I don't want no cold iron shackles
They hurts my pride, they hurts my pride.

J. & A. Lomax, "Take This Hammer" ©

Wash knew a good steak house in St. Francisville, so we detoured a bit to find it. St. Francisville was a very pretty town, and it seemed to have a church about every other block. The steaks were top sirloin and the best we'd had so far. I told Wash quietly that I'd like to visit a church, and he told me just as quietly to go right ahead. I slipped out to the car, got Cornelia's prayer book, and found the Catholic church about two blocks down. It was mostly white and blue, with two statues of the Blessed Virgin and an ornate white-and-gold main altar.

I opened Cornelia's book at random and came upon one of the finest prayers I've ever read. I learned later that it was part of the Episcopal communion service, but I firmly believe that when you find a good thing you use it. So, after reading it over, I knelt down and prayed it like a good Protestant.

"We do not presume to come to thy Table, O merciful Lord, trusting in our own righteousness, but in thy manifold and great mercies. We are not worthy so much as to gather up the crumbs under thy Table. But thou art the same Lord whose property is always to have mercy. Grant us, therefore, gracious Lord, so to eat the flesh of thy dear Son Jesus Christ, and to drink his blood, that we may evermore dwell in him, and he in us. Amen."

I was perfectly well aware that I wasn't receiving communion at the time, but I thought of the fine beefsteak I'd just had and offered it up as a salutary substitute.

When I got back to the restaurant, there was an argument between Sonny Bliss and Lieutenant March over the check. March said we'd been charged for eleven steaks, but there were only ten dirty plates. Sonny said Mose had ordered his steak, but then left for the men's room before he was served and hadn't returned. The missing steak was found in the kitchen, being kept warm. The question then was what the hell had happened to Mose. We checked the men's room and the cars; no trace of Mose.

And there came a point when Wash and I simultaneously looked at one another, and Wash said, "Goddamn. Angola Annex. How far is it?"

"Just down the road."

"He's gone to see his daddy."

"What?" said March. "Has he gone AWOL? I mean, he's got to follow regulations."

"Well," Wash said, "just for now, he's followin' his heart."

The guard at the Angola Annex gate looked at me with some astonishment. "What the hell these Niggra people to you?"

"I'm their lawyer."

"In a military uniform?"

"Adjutant General's Office. Sergeant," I said to Wash, "would you get my credentials folder out of the trunk?"

Wash looked at me, half-grinning. "Yeah, and I'll inform Lieutenant March of our difficulty." Wash headed straight for March, who was approaching with his mouth open.

"No difficulty, no difficulty," said the guard. "These other people prisoner chasers?"

"That's right."

"Well, there was a boy here just a while back, askin' after one of our prisoners."

"Which one was that?"

He consulted a clipboard. "Askin' after Prisoner Oates, Artemus Q. Number six, six—"

"And what did you tell him, Officer?"

"Told him Oates, Artemus Q., was over in Clinton on a roof tar detail, and that there's no way he could visit with him."

"Did you tell him why?"

"Told him he got to get written permission from the warden, sometimes the governor, when you got a murderer-lifer. And *that* can take six months, a year."

"You've been a great help, Officer. I'll see that you're mentioned in my report."

"Why thank you, sir. Name's Alvin Brand. That's Br—"

"Got it. Have to get cracking. Thanks again."

It wasn't hard to find the hot tar roofing detail in Clinton. There was a big, medieval-looking tarpot on wheels in front of a bank building, ladders on the side of the building, and about seven fat-bellied guards armed with short-snout pump shotguns. The smoke and stink and heat of the adjacent air was barely tolerable, and the Angola boys—all black and all equipped with mops—were up on the roof in the hot sun, in the intense heat off the tar, heat so bad that the best of crews can only stand it for five or six minutes. I'd hot-tarred a couple of chickenhouse roofs in my time on the farm, and I could still feel it in my feet.

We pulled up in some small shade and looked around for Mose.

"There he is," said Wash, pointing to a tree in the bank parking lot.

March came up alongside our car. "There he is, Sergeant. Under that tree. Are you going to arrest him, or shall I?"

"Nobody's going to arrest him," Wash said, climbing out. "He had my permission."

"Oh. Well, you didn't inform me of that."

"Lots of things I don't inform you about, *sir*! Like my bowel movements."

"What? What did you say?"

I'd slid out behind Wash. "Fowl movements, sir." I winked at him. "Yardbird talk."

"Oh," he said, looking perfectly blank. "Well, if you gave him permission—"

"Yes, sir. Thank you, *sir*!" Wash said, and nodded for me to follow him.

The chief guard was sitting on a box under an oak tree, smoking a cigarette. But we got to Mose first. He was standing, staring up, tears running down his face.

"Which one is he, Mose?" Wash asked.

"The big one, sergeant. With the bandanna."

"You talked to him yet?"

"They won't let me. Said he'd shoot both of us."

"Who said that?"

"The man, over there, with the big hat."

"Yeah," Wash said. He glanced at me. "Have to talk to that man."

"You wait here, Mose," I said. "You are by God going to talk to your daddy."

"Thanks, Cully."

We went over to the chief guard. He made, at first, as if he didn't see us.

"Sergeant," I said to Wash. "Tell this man who we are."

"Yes, sir," Wash said. "We from the Adjutant General's Office."

The chief guard glanced around. "He ain't talkin' to no prisoner."

"That right?" said Wash, going to his wallet. "If you say so, of course, we got to honor your position." Wash put a bill in his hand, folded. "My name's Washington. Master Sergeant C. George Washington." Wash extended his hand. "United States Air Force Adjutant General's Office."

The chief guard threw down his cigarette, stamped it out, but still didn't reach for Wash's black hand. I said, "The adjutant general would take it very kindly if you were to allow this airman to speak to his father. You see, the young man hasn't long to live. He's got leukemia. Service connected, of course."

By now the Angola boys were scrambling down the ladders for a break. The chief guard looked from me to Wash's hand, then hesitantly reached out and took it. He felt the bill, looked down at it. A fifty. He glanced up quickly at Wash.

"Mean that much, does it?"

"It surely do."

The chief guard thought upon it—for a good five seconds. "Okay," he said. "Five minutes. And I'll be right here, watchin'. No touchin', no huggin', or I may have to shoot."

"Yes, sir," Wash said, turning at once and crossing to Mose. Wash brought Mose back, explaining the rules as he came. Then the chief guard got to his feet, picked up his shotgun, and shouted, "Oates! Over here, on the run!"

Mose's father, who hadn't seen Mose yet, turned, went into an immediate trot. Halfway across to us, he recognized Mose, and came almost to a full stop. Then he left out a whoop, and started to sprint toward Mose. The chief guard stepped between them, fired two shots in the air.

"No goddamned touchin'!" he shouted. "Three feet apart, hands visible at all times!"

And so it was. And I don't think I've witnessed a more heart-breaking business in my life. The two men standing, straining toward one another, the tears and sweat of that strain pouring down their faces, their eyes locked, their pain throbbing between them so that it was almost audible.

I backed way, into shade, so I didn't hear what they said after Mose's "I love you, daddy." Even Wash—who was standing right next to the chief guard—had to look away, back off a step or two.

The chief guard didn't give them five minutes; not even two. As soon as it was time for the crew to go back up on the roof, he delivered a low, snarling grunt. "That's it! Up on the roof! Let's go!" As Mose's father backed away and turned toward the bank, the chief guard glanced around at Wash. "Gave 'em all the slack I could."

"You're all heart," Wash said. He went over, put one arm around Mose, led him away, saying: "Come on, son. We got to tend to business."

Mose quietly wept all the way to Lafayette.

FIFTEEN

They came a time for those young men
to get blooded.
And, Lordy Lord, did we ever
arrange it.

Ace Kingdom

We turned right at Baton Rouge for Lafayette. It was all cotton country, and soybeans, and hotter than the hammers of hell. Wash felt buoyant: he was heading into home country and was planning a big lunch for us the next day in New Iberia. Wash thought he knew exactly where we were going, but when we got there, it was just an empty field full of drain water.

"Shee-it," he said. "Got flooded out."

We stopped at a pool hall on the southside of town where Wash got a handwritten map from some old buddies. It looked like hen tracks to me, and I said so.

"It's bayou for sure," Wash said. "Mosquitoes big as your peckerhead."

"Why in the bayou?"

"Cops clampin' down. Somebody got killed last month over to Breaux Bridge."

We came out of a tunnel of overhanging underbrush, trees

draped with Spanish moss and kudzu, and there seemed to be a splotch of light well ahead.

"We lost, Cully?" Coop asked.

"Well, lost might be overstating it."

"We lost," Chappie said flatly.

"I smell snakes," Sonny said.

"What's this one, Wash? Another crap shoot?"

"No. This one on the up and over. We could get real healthy here."

The light had been growing, and suddenly we were there—a clearing in a cane field with a ring set up in the middle, an automobile drawn up on each side with the headlights on, and the considerable crowd packed in around the cars. The whole outer perimeter was covered with cars and pickups and motorcycles. The bleachers—planks on wooden boxes—were packed, and there was already some kind of a chant going—in Cajun, Wash said—which was more or less saying let's get this damn show on the road. Most of the men appeared to have rolls of dollar bills clutched in their hands, giving the appearance of a cockfight crowd. There were two makeshift shacks at the far end of the field, and we could see black men—big, older-looking black men—going in and out of one of them.

Wash drove toward the shacks, heaved a long sigh: "Well, young gentlemen, it looks like we goin' to earn our money tonight."

We were spotted as we closed toward the shacks, and a good-natured cheer went up. Most of the crowd rose, waved their fists full of money, and a ragtag Cajun band struck up "Hot Tamale Baby."

"They tryin' Buckwheat Zydeco, and it ain't good," Wash said.

"Jesus," Coop said. "East Asshole, Louisiana."

"But they friendly," Sonny said.

Two men in front of the empty shack were waving us over, and we parked in front of it.

"Hey! You find us pretty good!"

The rest of the conversation was mostly in unintelligible Cajun, which Wash handled like a native. We were shown into the empty shack, while Wash was escorted to the other to oversee hand taping and other details.

Our shack was obviously used for storing field equipment and other amenities. There was drinking water, buckets of slop water, basins on makeshift tables, and a half-assed field toilet hanging on one wall. There were spikes to hang our clothes on, and a stack of washcloths that, we rightly assumed, would have to serve us instead of a shower.

There were two other remarkable things. First was a brand new scale, set up on its own pedestal—the kind you find in boxing gyms. The other, in a back corner, laid edge up over a pair of sawhorses, was a rack of machetes, some two dozen, all so beautifully honed and polished that they might have been a museum display.

Chappie picked one up. "Goddamn," he said. He tested it with his thumb and drew blood. "Cane cutters," he said. "They be cane cutters."

"That bad?" Coop said.

"They very tough men. Most from Cuba. We got troubles."

Wash came in then, pouring sweat, looking worried. "Listen up here now. I just been over watchin' their man wrap hands. He be here in a minute to watch me. And weigh you out. He's a very professional man. From Cuba. And so are his fighters. I mean, they're amateurs by the rules, but they professional by the looks. And they are men, twenty-five, twenty-eight, and they got the hands and the eyes of real hard cases." He looked around at us and spoke almost paternally. "Up to now, you fought good. I been proud of you. But we been fightin' mostly boys. *And* we been fightin' white. You know what I mean. Don't try to hurt . . . *bad.* Well now, we goin' to fight black. Mean, hard, like it's your *life*. Or *his*. Because you can die out there, you know. Or, you can kill." A pause. "Take your choice, because tonight you're goin' to find out what you made of."

There was a shocked silence. Wash seemed to wait for some question or wisecrack, but there was none.

A soft knock on the door broke the silence. Wash opened to Lieutenant March and a man who looked Hispanic.

"This is our team," he said to the man. "Gentlemen, this is Mr. Gomez, the Cuban manager."

Gomez got right to work with Wash, taping directly to the skin (no chance of plaster of paris here), and writing down the precise weights in the given categories. I weighed in at one sixty-two, but Gomez waived it with a nod to Wash. It was all briskly done, and Gomez smiled and bowed his way out. We were dumbstruck.

"Jesus, Wash," Coop said. "You got us all shook up."

"Meant to," Wash said. "Goin' to be a hard night."

"Hell," Waldo said, "they cain't but beat us up. I mean, I ain't dyin' in this asshole place for nobody."

We laughed, felt a little better. Then, from the rear of the shack, March spoke. "What on earth is this?"

He was standing over the rack of machetes.

"Machetes," Spider said. "Cuban cane knives."

"My God. What if there's a disturbance? They're very volatile you know."

"Don't sweat it," Wash said wearily.

"Well, somebody has to stand guard on these weapons," March said. "I'd best go out and get my side arm."

And Lieutenant March, in a first display of anything like courage, hurried out of the shack.

Wash looked after him, shook his head. Then he raised his

eyes to heaven: "Side arm. That silly bastard couldn't hit Jesus Christ from the foot of the cross with a scattergun."

There was a roar of laughter. Despite himself, Wash had managed to send us out to face the Cubans smiling and giggling, which seemed to disconcert locals and Cubans alike.

But Wash, as usual, had the thing pretty well estimated. The Cubans were seated in a row on one side of the ring, and a plank had been cleared for us to do the same. The Cubans had taken their shirts off, and, though it had stopped raining, sat there in the humid air with their chests, and abs, and heavy shoulders gleaming. As soon as we were seated, Coop stood up and peeled off his shirt, and the rest of us followed suit. The noise in the crowd was growing louder and continuous, in English, French, Cajun, Creole, and Spanish. The Cuban nonfighters, about twenty of them, were especially noisy but good-natured and having a ball.

Spider was up first, and as soon as he climbed into the ring across from the Cuban, the betting started. On all three white sides the betting broke out with shouts and argument and some pushing and shoving. The black side, including the Cuban contingent, was relatively quiet. This continued throughout the match. Maybe they just didn't have much money to bet.

Spider's man was ten years older and had a bolo punch. It was sudden, vicious, and almost untelegraphed. Spider went down at forty-five seconds and again at one-fifty-four of the first round. He came out under his own power. "Lord Christ, Cully," he said. "if he's a bantam, I'm Tiger Larrabee."

Stone won his first round on points but got tagged in the second and went down like a suspiring sack of wheat. Later he said, "I thought sledgehammers were outlawed."

Sonny finished his fight, but got a bad eye cut, a split lip, and a bruise on his right cheekbone the size of a Granny Smith apple. He lost on points.

Waldo came dancing out with his fast hands moving about twice as fast as his feet, kept it up for three rounds, and his opponent never laid a serious glove on him. "Boss," he said to me later, "I gave him my West Virginia reel, and he was dancin' the rhumba." They called it a draw.

Mose's fight was scratched by mutual consent.

I knocked my man down twice in the second round with power rights, but he overtook me in the third. He was an "arm" expert, and I could hardly hold my arms above my waist. He pounded me pretty good, had me out on my feet. I didn't go down, and he got an honest decision. Wash protested that he was wearing six-ounce gloves. He wasn't. His hands were just so damned big they outsized the gloves.

Coop fought the semi-main against a first-class slugger. He hit Coop a heart shot in the first round that Coop thought had collapsed his lungs. Coop turned on the speed, and the man's head looked like a prime rib roast by the end of the fight. Incredibly, they also called this one a draw.

Chappie got a huge two-hundred-forty-pound man who moved beautifully—for about the first forty seconds. He did hit Chappie three right hands that obviously hurt. But then Chappie clinched, broke clean, and brought a left hook that sounded like buckshot hitting a cantaloupe. The Cuban fought on for about six seconds, then fell over, hitting the canvas like a great side of gristle. Later, Chappie thought he might be bleeding internally, and he did spit up a lot of blood, but it eased up by nightfall.

Four losses, two draws, and a knockout win. The money wasn't too good, but Wash was just glad we'd gotten out alive. I was bleeding again from the right ear, the upper lip, a cut over my left eye, and split-cuts on both elbows. I also had three loose teeth and a high whistling in my ears. My Cuban opponent came over (they all did) to congratulate us. He spoke a little English, so I thanked him for being generous about my overweight problem. He grinned and said, "Oh, me too! Fifteen pound!" He slapped his iron stomach: "All right here!"

I smiled and shook hands. My own stomach was ringing like a hot bell. Which is what happens when you fight heavyweights.

We went to a Cajun restaurant in Lafayette for dinner. We all sat at one long table, looking like surgical ward patients on an outing. Ace sat at one end of the table, Lieutenant March sat in the middle (still wearing his side arm, to which he had apparently become attached), and I sat at the far end. There was a Cajun band playing loudly in one corner of the large dance floor and a huge, stuffed alligator on a room divider just abaft my left ear. Its mouth was wide open, and every now and then I would pour a slosh of beer into it. Everyone was drinking beer—a special dispensation—but I hadn't got the hang of it yet, and the alligator seemed to love it. Wash was off tending to business, paying the doctor who had stitched us all up.

The band was playing Cajun standards. I wrote some of the titles down. "Tasso/McGee's Reel," "My Baby Don't Wear Shoes," "High Point Two Step," "Zydeco 'Round the World," "La Valse de Pont d'Amour," "Zydeco Cha Cha," "Juste une Reve," "Acadie a la Louisiane," "Sa M'Appel Fou," "Parlez-Nous a Boire," and God knows what all else. There were people singing and dancing, and a lot of yelping and hooting in the Cajun manner. Coop was soon yelping and hooting along with Waldo and Chappie. We had been strictly warned not to attempt to dance with the ladies. It would lead to sudden trouble, the manager said, making a stabbing motion with his social finger. He'd let us in after some discussion, and the fact that we were the boxers who had performed earlier out in the bayou overcame the fact that we were black.

Wash finally came walking in from the rear area, and I moved over to give him the head of the table. He was grinning happily, and immediately dinged for quiet as the band concluded a set.

"Okay," Wash said, "turn up your ear phones." We quieted, and he looked around at us. "My God, you are the sorriest lookin' bunch of privates I seen since my last pecker check." We tried to laugh, but we had to be careful of our lip stitches. "Now," Wash said. "We too busted up to fight in New Iberia. And we ain't goin' to be much better for Avery Island. So . . . I called them both off." We *were* able to cheer. "In fact, Iberia and Avery goin' to fight each other night after tomorrow."

Chappie said, "That's a three-day pass!"

"That's a three-day pass all the way into New Orleans," Wash said.

"But we goin' to lose a couple paydays," Sonny said.

"Don't worry that," Wash said. "I got me a small fee for fixin' up the Iberia-Avery fight. They normally too damned mad at each other to fight, but I arranged it."

I could sense there was something bigger he had to say, and he finally got to it.

"Somethin' else," he said grinning. "We got us *real* healthy tonight. Little wager I made." He waited.

"What the hell, Wash? You bet on the Cubans?"

"Would I do that?" Wash said over the laughter. "No, sir. I had me a little premonition. So . . . I bet the whole wad on Tony Zale." He waited again, grinning. "And he stiffed Rocky Graziano in six in Chicago."

We cheered just as the band struck up, and Wash sat down looking like the happiest man in Lafayette Parish.

How the hell Coop had the time and the energy that night to find a woman I can't fathom, but he did. He brought her in about an hour after I'd gone to bed. We had, thank God, twin beds, and I went into my usual drill, scrunched over against the wall with my fingers to my ears, trying not to hear the squeals and whispers and the rhythmic thumping of the other bed against the wall.

At long last it was over, and I was slipping back into sleep when Coop came over to my bed and laid a heavy hand on my back.

"Hey, man."

"What?"

"Listen. I don't know how to tell you this, but she was at the fight, and she says she'll do you for nothin'."

I hit him with the back of my right arm, and he fell off the bed and lay there, knotted with laughter.

Then the girl said, "Hey, stud. You goin' to walk me home, or ain't ya?"

I caught a glimpse of her—tall, very pretty, mahogany skin—and then rolled to the wall and started to say a prayer. But then I got to laughing and fell asleep wondering if my vocation to the priesthood was going to survive this damned trip.

A great day, and we lit out for the Big Easy with Lowell Fulson on the radio singing "Rollin' Blues" and Chappie on the backseat with his guitar trying to keep up. Chappie was now composing a song entitled "You Have Had Your Piece of Me," using the melody of "Just a Closer Walk with Thee." All he was sure of so far by way of lyric was the couplet: "Jesus, woman, cain't you see? You have had your piece of me!" Pretty damn good stuff, I thought, for a country boy.

We'd had a big breakfast, but we weren't ten miles down the road when Sonny went dry.

"Hey, Wash," he said. "I'm dyin' of the thirst."

"Bad for you," Wash said.

"Dyin' of anythin' is bad for you," Coop said.

"I mean all the damn liquid. Best you lean and dry."

I said, "There's a store coming up. Says . . . Moon Pie and Royal Crown Cola."

"Oh, my Lord," said Chappie. "Moon Pie and R.C.!"

"We could use some gas, Wash," I said.

"Bunch of goddamned swill bellies," Wash said, but he slowed the car and I gave Ace the piss-stop signal.

We pulled in slowly. No gas pumps. Just the store with a long porch, six or seven rocking chairs, each occupied by local young men in overalls, straw hats, and bandannas, and each holding a bottle of beer. Wash came to a stop in front of the porch.

"Mornin'!" he said. "Store open? Thought we'd buy some Moon Pies and sody pop!"

No response. Not a discernible twitch. Then, after a long silence, two of the men got out of their chairs. Then a third. They came forward to the porch steps, walked down almost solemnly, came around the front of our car, ignoring Wash, and came up on the passenger side, staring at me.

"Good morning," I said. "The store open?"

All three pushed their hats back on their heads, bent over slightly, peered in at me. They gave me a long, careful inspection.

"Well, what the hell you think we got here, Jimmy Bob?" one of them said.

"Well it do look sort of white, Billy Ray," Jimmy Bob said.

"It *is*, by God, sort of white," Billy Ray said. "Like you sometimes get a white turd."

"You know what I think it is?"

"What's that, Rudy Dee?"

"I think it's a goddamn USDA prime nigger lover."

All three nodded, pulled at their noses and bottles.

I turned to the backseat. "Hey, Coop," I said.

"Yeah."

"I think there's enough for both of us."

I slammed my front door open, right into Billy Ray's face, hit Rudy Dee full in the mouth, and the fight was on.

The porch emptied, both cars emptied, Lieutenant March took to his heels, Wash and Ace were engaged immediately, so that it was a full team effort from the start, and the locals never really had a chance. Jimmy Bob and I had a bit of a go—he was two hundred pounds and country hard—until he backed into Chappie, and Chappie turned and decked him with a short right. I was looking around for another partner when I saw somebody hit Wash over the head with a short hoe handle. Wash disarmed him, picked him up, and threw him under one of the cars. I peeled a fat guy off Tremaine, who'd simply gotten fallen on, and hooked him one in the belly. He grabbed it with both hands, sat down, and said, "Shitfire." Then I saw that Waldo had two going at once, and I went over and cut in. I got a raw-boned redhead with a big grin. He was enjoying himself. Meanly, I decided to remove some of his grin. My second right hand knocked out some teeth on the left side. He spit them out, started spitting blood, looked at himself in the rear view mirror of one of the cars, and started to cry. "Oh Jesus," he said, "my mother will kill me."

It didn't last very long, maybe three minutes, and then there came a strange quiet. There were seven civilians on the ground. The Air Force was still standing. I looked across to Wash. "I think we'd better get the hell out of here," I said.

And, with March sprinting for his car at the last moment, we did.

We were proceeding at legal speed toward Thibodeaux not two minutes later when a police car, sirens blaring, went whizzing past us in the other direction. Somebody had telephoned the cops, and I suspected Lieutenant March immediately but didn't say anything.

Then Wash said, "I saw that little weasel on the phone, in the outside booth."

"You think he's capable of that?"

"Hell, yes."

"Can we get rid of him?"

"Sure. I telephone the Secretary of the Air Force soon as we gets in."

Wash laughed, and I said, "We can certainly telephone the colonel."

"That's what I had in mind," Wash said. "And you do it, with me dialin' for you. For the good of the service."

Being flush and eager for some tender, loving care, we determined to stay at the best hotel that would have us. Wash had once dined at the Pontchartrain Hotel in the Garden District, and he thought they might receive us without bullshit. So we stopped in the town of Westwego and I telephoned the Pontchartrain Hotel. They were very courteous, and when I told them that we were a United States Air Force team of technical specialists in town on a quite confidential mission, they (the day manager and the reservations manager) offered a 30 percent discount, and said they would hold six rooms for us until eight o'clock that night. I thanked them and was about to hang up when I heard the day manager say, "Of course, Captain Madden, your team is all white?" I hung up.

I didn't say anything to Wash about the all-white business, but when we got to the hotel I collared Lieutenant March.

"Sir, I want you to come to the desk with me."

"Why, of course. We have finally lighted upon a proper hotel."

"Sir, I want you to let me do the talking. Is that all right with you?"

He looked at me. "I am perfectly capable—"

"I know what you're capable of, sir. Just indulge me this once."

"Well, airman, if there is some good reason."

"There is an excellent reason, sir. I'll explain later."

"Very well, Madden. But I reserve the right—"

"Of course you do."

March and I went to the desk. March, uncomfortably, kept his mouth shut, even when they addressed me as captain. I paid for the six rooms in advance with the cash that Wash had given me. Then I fixed the clerk and the day manager with a stern eye. "You will almost certainly get a call from the New Orleans Police Department concerning arrangements for our team's safety. If they do not call, that will be in the interest of security. But I hope a small police presence will not be an inconvenience."

"Oh, no sir. We understand. We will cooperate fully."

"Thank you. Now, we will need several bellboys with heavy duty carts."

"Yes, sir." He banged on a bell. I took March by the elbow, guided him toward the front door.

"What in God's name was that all about?"

"That was about getting nine black airmen checked into a New Orleans hotel, sir."

"But I'm sure if you'd just told the truth—"

"Wherein did I lie, sir?"

"Well, all that about the New Orleans police."

"No lie, sir. I fully intend to call them. You've seen how we have been severally attacked without provocation?"

"Well, yes, I suppose so. But we should call military police, if anybody."

"I've already done that, sir. I wouldn't be surprised if we are even now under surveillance."

"Airman Madden. I have to protest your going over my head. This is perhaps the third or fourth time that you—"

"It's the fifth, sir," I said. "But I can assure you it will not happen again. The next time will be right at your head, sir. Tête-à-tête, as it were."

"All right then. I would appreciate it."

Wash and the team were still waiting in the cars. I passed out keys, told them to go into the lunch room, order, eat, and then one by one to make their way up to their rooms. We'd sort the baggage out later.

It worked to perfection. Whenever the manager asked me about when the team would arrive, I'd wink and say it was all clandestine, and that he really shouldn't notice. Then I'd ask him, in the interest of security, please to address me as airman. He was the soul of discretion, and winked at me in return. To this day I don't know if the Pontchartrain would have taken us in straight up, but it was too much fun the other way even to have risked it. The manager had found out about the black men by the next morning, but to his credit all he said to March was, "We are pleased that you chose the Pontchartrain as your base for your secret mission." March told me that he replied: "What secret mission?" And that the manager had replied: "Just as you say, sir." And that the manager had winked at him.

⌞⌝⌞⌝⌞⌝

We were in the Garden District and, as luck would have it, not far from Miss Chamberlin's Seminary.

"So what are you going to do?" Coop asked.

"I can't take it to her looking like this," I said.

"Sure you can. Wounded man in uniform. Ladies just roll right over."

"I think I'll just mail it to her."

"Hell, you will! If I got to drag you over there!"

"Coop, have you looked in the mirror lately?"

"Just a minute ago."

"Well, you got a fat mouth."

"Always have had."

"I mean, you look beat up."

"Listen, Catfish, I already called my girl."

"Your girl. You've got a girl?"

"I already told you I had a girl. Lainie."

"Yeah, but I didn't believe you. Not after all those . . . other girls."

Coop, who was doing his ab exercises, burst out laughing. "Goddamn! Am I goin' to get me the short chastity sermon?"

"The long one."

"Cully. *Fi*-delity, as you calls it, is a two-way street, right?"

"It should properly be, yes."

"Well, my man, wait till you see Lainie!"

And he burst out laughing, rolled around on the floor, kicking his feet. "Wait'll you see Lainie!"

"I don't know what you're talking about."

"And I don't know what you talkin' about! And neither does Lainie know what you talkin' about! And *you* don't know what you talkin' about!"

"I certainly do."

"Cully, do you think Lainie's been waitin' for me faithful all this time?"

"If she loves you."

"Love me? Hell yes, she love me. But that don't mean she been puttin' staples on her crotch the whole time I'm gone! I mean, she's human, Cully, and she got her *needs*!"

I looked at him in some small astonishment. "You mean, other men?"

"No, no!" he shouted, laughing and rolling joyously. "I mean other raccoons!"

I knew I was being stupid, or suspected I was, but I was damned if I'd accept this kind of moral bollix. Like certain owls, I believed in mating for life, and that, if you went around inserting yourself into random females, you were no better than a rutting hog. I believed this. I truly did. But what the hell did I know?

Coop calmed down and looked at me with something like pity. "Cully, you got to understand that the world don't run strictly by the Ten Commandments. It don't even come close."

"That doesn't make it right."

"How do you know that? It may be the rightest thing about the world."

"Don't you believe in God?"

"Sure I believe in God. And I believe in the way He made me."

"Do you believe in Jesus Christ?"

"Sure I do. I use his name all the time."

"But he lived and preached a chaste life."

"Two thousand years back. Maybe them people hadn't got the rhythm of things yet."

"Oh for God's sake, Coop, Jesus was not just a man of his times, He was divine. He invented the rhythms of the universe. You can't—"

There came a knock at the door. I opened to Wash, a splendid figure of a man in his very best uniform.

"Ace and I are goin' over to the New Orleans Boxing Club, to talk to the man. You two want to come along?"

"Hell yes." I looked around at Coop. "You got other plans?"

"No. Lainie don't get off till four."

"You got ten minutes."

The New Orleans Boxing Club was a mosquelike building, white with blue trim, with its name in gold lettering arched over the wide front door, and beneath it the legend "House of Champions." There were offices on either side of the front door. Wash led us to the left side where we discovered "the man"—a fat, white disaster in a white suit and hat, who easily could have played Will Varner. His name was—I swear to God—Tookie Snodgrass.

"Sergeant Washington," he said. "New Orleans is honored."

Wash introduced us, we all took seats opposite Tookie, and Wash got right to it. "I want a thousand show-up fee, fifty at the bell for each match, and an additional hundred for each win."

You'd have thought he just shot Tookie in the belly button. "Ee-yow!" he said. "You will put me out of business! I don't have that many seats!"

"You got standin' room," Wash said. "But I tell you what I'll do. My man loses, no fifty dollars. So, I mean, your people beat up on us, I walk out with just the show-up thousand. Now you can't get it any fairer than that."

Tookie was doing his arithmetic. "Yeah, but say you win all eight fights, that's twelve hundred plus the show-up is twenty-two hundred which means I make a huge two-fifty on the evening."

"Bite your tongue," Wash said. "You do three rows of ringside at ten per, that's four times twenty-four is ninety-six hundred, plus twenty-five hundred on the rest of the house, and you's lookin' at thirty-four sixty, which means—even if we win all eight, which ain't likely, your referees bein' what they are—you walk away with twelve hundred sixty."

"Yeah, but I got overhead. The referees, the handlers, the cut men, security. You wouldn't believe how it adds up."

"And then, of course," Wash said, "You got the hot dog and beer and popcorn and sody pop, which probably nets you up to two grand on a hit night."

"Well, I can't figure that in. And I haven't even mentioned advertising."

"Yeah, right. I saw that ad today in the *Times-Picayune*. A full inch square. Must have cost you eighty-three cents."

Tookie sat back, heaved a windy sign, took out a handkerchief and wiped his forehead. "Can't do it, sergeant."

"Okay," Wash said, getting to his feet. "Then the Air Force cancels. No fights tomorrow night."

Tookie looked up at him. "You'd do that to me? I mean, I've got this fight sold out." He caught himself, bit at his lower lip.

Wash grinned. "Figured you did. Have we got a deal?"

Tookie shook his head. "You're a very hard man."

"I stays alive."

Then, with a scrunching of his face in pain, a twisting of his body—obscene, as if someone were reticulating his rectum—Tookie moaned: "You've got a deal."

He extended his hand to Wash. Wash shook it. Wash said, "Done."

"Done," said Tookie, making a complete, remarkable recovery. "How's that gym you got in New Iberia?"

"Nailed up tight. But it's waitin' for me."

"We'll do a little business when you get operatin'."

"We just might do that," Wash said.

As we went out to the car, I said, "Wash, I'm amazed."

"I ain't."

"You expected to get that much?"

"Yeah."

"C'mon."

"Look, he say no, he be a dead man. The mob people want this fight, and he got to deliver it."

"The mob?" I said, blinking sunlight.

"Nice people. They run New Orleans like a slot machine. You want yo' sweet life, you just keep pullin' that handle."

SIXTEEN

I'm gon' get up in the mornin'
I believe I'll dust my broom
Girl friend, the black man you been lovin'
girlfriend, can get my room.

Robert Johnson, "I Believe I'll Dust My Broom"

Some minutes later, we were parked in front of Miss Chamberlin's Seminary. It was a mansion, imposing, with an iron fence around it, and a yard full of fine trees and garden paths lined with flowers. It took me a moment to realize where we were.

"What are we stopping here for?" I said, looking at the discreet little brass sign to one side of the gate.

"So you can give the nice lady her prayer book."

"I didn't bring the prayer book."

"I did," Coop said.

And he handed it forward to me. "Damn it, Coop. I'm not ready to go in there."

"Now come on," Wash said. "We go to all the trouble of findin' the address and all, ridin' you over here . . . the least you can do is go in and give her the book."

"But, Wash, I look like I've been hit by a truck."

"Tell her you're a boxer. She'll understan'."

"She'll scream."

"She's a lady, and ladies don't scream. They smile and they say thank you very much for my prayer book, and would you like to take me out for a sody pop."

"Oh God."

"You got any money?"

"No. I loaned it all to Coop."

Wash got out his wallet. "Here's ten. Now you take that young lady *down*-town!"

"To the hotel," Coop said.

"Shut your face," Wash said to Coop. "Now, go along, Cully. Be real nice to her. Take the street car. Treat her like a queen."

"Okay, Wash. Might as well get it over."

"Get it anyway you can," Coop said, grinning.

"Cooper, you shut up. I hit you one upside the head."

"Yes sir," Coop said. "Sergeant, *sir*!"

"Go along now, Cully."

"Thanks Wash. I'll see you back at the hotel."

I climbed out, slammed the door behind me. Wash drove off immediately, and there I was at the gate. I pushed at it and it swung open, and I took the long walk to the front door. I waited a minute, straightened my hat, then lifted the brass knocker and struck two soft blows. The door was snatched open by a young girl with great gray horn-rimmed glasses and a smile full of steel braces.

"Hi," she said. "I'm Prissy. Who are you?"

"My name is Cully Madden, and I've come to return this prayer book to Miss Cornelia Ellsworth. May I see her?"

"You certainly may not!" came a voice from an inner room. And the speaker came in at once, a woman in her seventies with a pince-nez, an imperious eye, and short-heeled shoes that made sounds on the wooden floor like pistol shots. The redoubtable Miss Chamberlin, and no question. "What do you want of her?"

"It's all right, Miss Chamberlin," said Cornelia, coming out of an adjoining office. "This is the young man who was so nice to me in New Madrid."

"Well, he might have at least changed his bandages."

"I did, ma'am. Two or three times."

"Hello, Cully," Cornelia said. "How on earth did you find me?"

"Hello," I said, finding it difficult to speak. She was so beautiful and bright and shining that I felt like a turd on a stick.

"Were you mauled by an animal?" Miss Chamberlin said.

"You might say that," I said. Then I handed the prayer book to Cornelia. "It has your name and address in it."

"Oh, my!" she said. "I've been looking all over for this."

"You left it in the booth, at breakfast."

"Of course. But how good of you to go to all this trouble."

"I've been reading it now and then. There are . . . well, some things in it I'd like to talk to you about."

"Such as what?" said Miss Chamberlin.

"Well, there are some differences between Catholicism and Episcopalianism—"

"I should certainly hope so," Miss Chamberlin said.

I looked to Cornelia. "Is there any way we could be alone to talk?"

Cornelia picked it up admirably. "Why, I think so. Our church is just around the corner. What better place?"

"You're going to church with him?" Miss Chamberlin said.

"I can see that he is honestly interested in Episcopalianism," Cornelia said. "And, as you've taught us, Miss Chamberlin, we must all be catechists."

"Humph," said Miss Chamberlin. "Well, be back within the hour."

"Yes, Miss Chamberlin."

The old dreadnought turned and went back into her office. Cornelia ducked into her office for a big-brimmed straw hat, and we were out of there.

We never went anywhere near the church. With no discussion at all, we caught the streetcar, got off at the Pontchartrain, and were in the coffee shop within ten minutes. I had gained a little confidence as to women, watching Coop operate. I even thought I'd learned a bit about taking command. But I damned shortly learned that it was I who was in tow, not Cornelia. All she asked was where I was staying, and my marching orders were cut.

She smiled at me across the table. "This is very nice. I'd have a cup of tea."

I signaled the waiter with such panache as I could muster, and ordered the tea and an R.C. Cola for myself. She seemed impressed . . . well, at least comfortable. "You were sweet to return my prayer book."

"I did it because you're the most beautiful girl I've ever seen."

"Well, you certainly are direct. And I'm very flattered." She hesitated. "You know, I really don't know your name. I heard you introduce yourself to Prissy, but all I heard was Cully."

"Cully Madden."

"Well, Cully Madden, I'm very glad to see you again."

"Thank you. I know I don't look like much. We've been boxing."

"Why do you do it?"

"It beats cleaning toilets."

"I suppose it does. But surely you have other options."

"I could shoot my commanding officer."

"I don't understand."

"He ordered me to box. Because I got in a lot of fights. It's really not worth explaining, and I don't mind. I'm pretty good at it, and I've met an outstanding group of men. My teammates."

"Those colored boys?"

"Men. Colored men."

"Pardon me."

"I don't mean to be defensive about it, but if you could see the way we are treated. The way black men are treated in the South is a damned outrage."

"Where are you from?"

"Upstate New York. A farm on the Hudson River."

"Have you known many Negroes?"

"No. These are the first."

"You're angry, aren't you?"

"With good reason."

"Maybe we ought to talk about something else?"

"Sure. How about you? Have you always lived here?"

"No. Oh no. My father is in the Navy, and we've lived all over the place. Hawaii, China, the Philippines, and, of course, New Orleans."

"What does your father do?"

"Well, right now he teaches at the Naval War College in Newport, Rhode Island."

"He's an officer?"

"Yes. He's a rear admiral."

"Oh my God," I blurted.

"You don't hate all officers."

"No, I don't. But they don't seem to take to me."

"He *is* a strict disciplinarian."

"So am I, believe it or not. But not in the military sense."

"In what sense, then?"

"Well—" The waiter saved me, bringing our drinks.

She sipped her tea plain, and fixed me with her blue eyes. "You don't just mean the discipline of boxing?"

"No. But I . . . I'm not sure I want to talk about it."

"Talk about it," she said softly.

I heaved a long sigh. "Okay. I guess I might as well. I have been thinking about—no, I have determined to study for the priesthood. In the Roman Catholic Church." I watched her closely, and she didn't field this quite so easily as I thought she might.

"You're serious?"

"I think so. I have my doubts. Like right now. But I'm pretty sure I'm going to give it a try."

"You feel you have a vocation?"

"Most of the time. . . . Well, I've got something. Maybe it's just curiosity."

"Or maybe it isn't."

"I suspect I'll find out damned quick."

She smiled. "You said you were interested in the Episcopal church. Just a ploy?"

"Not entirely. I've heard that Episcopal priests are allowed to marry."

She started to giggle. "They are allowed to marry. But I have to say, Cully, that I can't imagine you as an Episcopal priest." She giggled some more. "You'd frighten them to death."

"I don't always look this beat up."

"I don't mean that. I mean . . . your intensity." She shook her head. "No, I think you're a Jesuit or nothing."

"My God, you come to judgments fast."

"I apologize if I've offended you."

"No. You're probably dead right on. Except that I'm thinking of the Augustinian Order."

"Oh?"

I shrugged. "I met one of their priests once. A very learned man. And I can't take on the Jesuits if I'm one of them."

"You don't like the Jesuits?"

"I think they're a bunch of manipulators. Pious frauds."

"Oh my. You are a firebrand."

"Well, it's easy to talk about. The reality will be something else."

And, at this moment, an interruption. The hotel manager came up to our table, nodded to Cornelia with something like a smile, then turned to me. "I've been in touch with your commanding officer at Scott Field, *Captain* Madden. You are a private, and your group is nothing but a boxing team. There is nothing clandestine about you."

"Right," I said. "I lied. To get my people, finally, into a decent hotel."

"Well, your candor is refreshing," he said. "But if you'd told the simple truth, I might well have admitted you anyway."

"Would you really? Somehow I doubt hell out of that."

"I'm going to allow you and your group to stay the night, Mr. Madden. But as of tomorrow morning, I'll need the rooms."

"Fair enough. I'm sure we can find a suitable fleabag somewhere. Meanwhile, I certainly hope our blackness hasn't rubbed off on your towels."

"Thank you, Mr. Madden. Tomorrow morning then, before ten."

He turned and walked away. Cornelia looked at me with her pretty mouth slightly open. "That is the rudest thing I've ever heard!"

"Par for the course, and far better than most. It ain't easy being black south of the line."

"You think of yourself as black?"

"Occupational hazard, I guess." Then: "No, it would be the

worst kind of presumption for me to think of myself as black. I've got no idea what it must really be like. If I talk black, I don't know what the hell I'm talking about."

At this moment, up walked Wash. He bowed in a courtly manner to Cornelia. "Please forgive the intrusion," he said. "I'm Sergeant Washington."

"I'm very pleased to meet you," she said, and they shook hands.

Wash turned to me. "We got problems."

"I know. The manager just bounced us from the hotel. As of tomorrow morning."

"Somehow I ain't surprised. I got a hotel connection down on Basin Street. No big deal. But the other problem is Tookie Snodgrass."

"Figures. After the deal you drove."

"He say we look beat up and he wants us to have physicals before he ratify the deal. And he wants to move the fights to a steamboat."

"He's a sleazeball."

"True for you. Now we goin' to meet in the lobby after lunch, then go on down to the boxing club. If you can find Coop, tell him."

"I'll find him. See you then."

Wash bowed to Cornelia as he left.

"What a nice man."

"The best."

"You think your fight is off?"

"Oh, they'll work something out. You ever been to a fight?"

"No."

"Would you like to?"

"I'm not sure. But if you're fighting, I think I . . . would go."

"Good. I'm not sure where or when yet, but I'll let you know. Can you get out?"

"Oh, I'll just say I'm going to a church social. We have them all the time. We're very ecumenical. You Catholics don't mind a white lie?"

"No, but we blacks do."

She looked at me and smiled. "I've got no answer to that one."

"Good. We'll have something to talk about the next time."

We got back to Miss Chamberlin's more than an hour late, but Miss Chamberlin was taking her nap, and we got away with it. She smiled at me as I left her, and said, "I'd love to see you again."

And I walked away striding, thinking that I had finally arrived in life.

SEVENTEEN

An' the blues fell mama's child
Tore me all upside down.

Robert Johnson, "Preachin' Blues
(Up Jumped The Devil)"

Tookie Snodgrass's examining physician looked like he'd just been dragged out of a Basin Street bar on a rope. He was wearing a dirty white suit, a black string tie, and a Panama hat that appeared to have been set on fire and then extinguished with a wet mop. But he was certified by the Louisiana Boxing Commission and the AAU and had documents to prove it.

He examined Mose last. Mose hadn't, of course, fought the Cubans, and was in great, if still morose, shape.

"Nothin' wrong with this boy," the doctor said. "Except he's the saddest son-of-a-bitch I ever seen."

"Watch your tongue," Wash said.

"Well, okay then. He's got a depression that'd kill a sucklin' hog."

We couldn't argue with that, and the doctor now turned and delivered his summation. "You got four men with possible concussions, one with heavy facial lacerations, and one with a very bad eye. The only ones I'd approve right now are . . . Waldrop—"

"Waldron," said Waldo.

"And Madden. And he's no rose."

"But we got to have three, Doc," Tookie said hopefully. "I'm fillin' out the card with some boys from over in Algiers. But they ain't but six of them."

"Well, then, if his eye goes down, I'll approve the light heavyweight. But the rest of them ain't fightin' here." He got up, staggering a little. "When's the fight against the Marines?"

"Next week early," Wash said.

"I'd be damned careful, Sergeant. These boys took an awful pasting from them Cubans. You just don't know what kind of internal injuries they might have." He put on his filthy hat, and as he went out turned back to say, "I, personally, wouldn't fight any one of them for a month."

Tookie looked around. "You heard the man."

"He just coverin' his official AAU ass," said Wash.

"Maybe, but I got to go along."

"How far?" Wash said. "What's it goin' to cost me?"

"About half," Tookie said. "And I'm bein' generous, Wash."

"We discuss this later," Wash said. "After I count the crowd."

Tookie shook his head, put on his scruffy hat, and went out.

Wash turned to us. "Now tune in. That doctor don't know much, especially about us. But what he do know is that this New Orleans club got some of the toughest boys south of Detroit. If we was in good health, no problem. But we ain't. And we need the rest before the Marines. Especially Chappie, who spent most of last night heavin' up his guts. And old Stone, this mornin', thought he was in Natchez." Wash paused, held up his hand against murmurs. "Now. We goin' to have to skip Monday night at the club. We lose some money, *but* somebody's social club has set up a exhibition for tomorrow afternoon on a steamboat. They call it a exhibition to get around the cops, but it's no walk in the tulips. Still, the money's almost as good as the Monday, and five of you will get a nice rest. Now them's the marchin' orders, and the horse's mouth has spoke."

"Do I get to fight?" Mose asked.

"No. You ain't there yet. Waldo's okay. They'll never notice. And Cully and Coop, *if* we can get that eye down."

"Of course we can get it down!" Coop said. "Give me a goddamn razor blade, and I'll do it myself."

"Hold your face. Sergeant Kingdom, prepare to cut. Cully and Waldo stand by. The rest of you go get a nap."

As the others filed out, more or less happily, I said to Coop, "You see Lainie yet?"

"Later," he said. "An' you comin' with me."

"You ready?" Wash asked Ace.

"Ready."

"Hold your head still," Wash said.

"Yes, daddy," Coop replied.

Ace walked to him and with one slice opened the eye. Ace slipped a towel into the spurting blood, but not before he got a good slosh of it in his face.

"Good God, Ace!" I said. "You got his eyeball."

"Hand me the alcohol," Ace said.

I handed him the alcohol, he poured some onto a cotton swab, and went to work on the eye. In seconds, the job was done. Ace turned to wash his hands, and began to whistle. I went over to Coop, took a close look. "I can't believe it. It looks almost normal."

"My mother always told me," Coop said. "When it comes to surgery, go to the best in the country."

Ace said: "That'll be five hundred dollars, Airman Cooper. Payable to my favorite charity."

"What's that?"

"Alcoholics Anonymous," Ace said, grinning.

"Okay, Airman Madden," Wash said. "Let's have a close look at your scalp. Sergeant Kingdom, shave his head."

"Oh, now wait a minute, Wash. It's just a bump."

Wash grinned, then laughed. "Just testing you for vanity, my man. Mizz Cornelia made a big impression. You goin' to see her again?"

"I'm going to invite her to the fight. If I can get a ticket for her."

"Hell, Cully. I'll send a car."

⌞⌝⌞⌝⌞⌝

Miss Chamberlin was awake, so I couldn't see Cornelia, but I left a note saying a car would call for her around 1 P.M.

Coop was waiting for me at the gate. "That was fast."

"The old battleax is guarding the drawbridge. I had to leave a note."

"That'll work."

"I hope so. I think."

"What do you mean, you think? You want her there, don't say you don't."

"I guess so."

"Man, you hooked. I never seen anybody hooked like you."

"Look, Coop, I'm the world's expert on how I feel, and I definitely do not feel hooked."

Coop wagged his grin at me. "Oh man, it's worse than I thought."

"Are we going to the French Quarter or aren't we?

"We goin'. We gone! C'mon!"

We sprinted to catch a St. Charles streetcar that had just stopped at a crossing. We caught it as it started to move again.

"This goes close to where Lainie works."

"What's she do?"

"Oh, she traps white men for a detective business."

"Traps them?"

"Yeah. She so damned good-lookin' she get anybody up to a hotel room. Then the camera guy comes runnin' in, pops a few flashbulbs, and, bingo, they's another *di*-vorce. Lainie's the best."

"Sounds like it."

"When I turn pro and get a little green, I'm goin' to marry her."

"Then she can quit her job."

"Hell no. It pays too good."

"Yeah, but—"

"I got this thing about kids. I want some. So's they look up at me and say 'My daddy's champion of the world.' Nothin' wrong with that."

"No. Nothing wrong with that."

We got off at Canal and crossed into the French Quarter and entered at Royal. I loved the place from the first minute. The old wooden gates and courtyards, the ornamented houses, the grillwork balconies, the wide-open bars and music joints, the bands already warming up for a hot Saturday night, the sidewalk horn players and street dancers—the whole atmosphere of carnival and debauchery. We passed one place where I saw nearly naked girls swinging on brass poles—dark and threatening dens of forbidden pleasure. I looked away quickly, while Coop lingered and smiled. Then he rejoined me, saying, "God-damn, Cully. It's good to be home."

"Is this your neighborhood?"

"No. We lived over in Elysian Fields. Then my father left home, and my mother died of a drug habit. I hardly knew her by the time she passed. Sad story." Then he grinned. "But now we almost to Lainie."

Her office was in an old, restored building across from the Sonesta Hotel. We went up some narrow stairs and there was a sign on the door: Wente Associates: Private Investigators.

We went in and the first thing I saw was Lainie, sitting behind a massive desk. She was an absolute beauty, and she leaped out of her chair at the sight of Coop. She crossed to us—long-legged, hazel-eyed, with stunning bosom and the kind of wide, white, dazzling smile that can light up a dark room. Coop folded her in his arms and they kissed. And kissed. I finally sat down in a wooden armchair and picked up a copy of *Good Housekeeping*. Coop noticed, and eased out of the kiss, and said, "Hey Lainie, I want you to meet Mr. Cully Madden, my roommate."

"Of course," she said.

"Cully this is Lainie."

She extended her hand, and I took it. "I've heard so much about you," she said.

"And I about you."

"Coop's letters are always Cully this, and Cully that," she said.

"You know, roomin' with a white man, they's always all kinds of things to complain about."

Lainie laughed, pure joy with the tone of a well-tempered saxophone. I studied her light coffee-colored skin, looking for a flaw or a wrinkle. She was perfect. Coop caught me at it.

"She pass inspection?"

"She certainly does."

"Think she could trap me in a hotel?"

"Cooper!" she said, but was still smiling.

"I'm delighted to meet you."

"Yeah," Coop said, "but what were you thinking?"

"I was thinking what beautiful children you two will have."

"What a lovely thing to say," Lainie said. She leaned in and gave me a quick kiss on the cheek.

"Children," Coop said in mock alarm. "Control your passions! We ain't even had supper yet!"

⌞⌝⌞⌝⌞⌝

We went to a place called Brennan's. Lainie seemed to have a lot of influence there, and we got the last table in a crowded dining room. I took one look at the menu, the prices, and rolled my eyes up at Coop.

"Don't worry," Coop said. "This is Lainie's treat."

"And about time," Lainie said, "You been away *forever*."

"I'll drink to that," Coop said. He turned to the waiter, whispered to him, and three drinks appeared on the table in nothing flat. Coop picked his up, toasted us both. "To the most gorgeous lady and the best friend a man could have."

I raised my glass, took a sip. It tasted smooth, but wickedly powerful, and I choked just a bit.

"Are you all right?" Lainie asked.

"Don't worry, Cully. This is called a Sazerac. It was invented by a white man, and it's good for whatever ails you. Including virginity."

"Virginity," Lainie said, looking at me. "Are you a virgin?"

"Yes," I said, feeling my face get hot.

"May I ask why?"

"He's a believer," Coop said. "A true believer."

"Oh, I don't know. I—"

"He thinks he wants to be a priest," Coop said.

"Is that right?" asked Lainie.

"He prays every night, on his knees. And every morning. I told you what it was like, living with a white man."

"Hush, Cooper." Then, to me, "You really are going to be a priest?"

"I've been thinking about it."

"Well, I think that's wonderful," she said.

We drank again, and I was beginning to feel it already.

"Am I being too personal?" Lainie said.

"No, no. It's just that my mind isn't really made up. Yet."

"Yeah," Coop said. "Think about it for at least eight years."

We all laughed, and ordered. Coop and I had one-pound New York steaks, and Lainie had the bouillabaisse with a glass of white wine. I've never had a better steak or a better time. Lainie suggested we have Bananas Foster with a snifter each of a hazelnut liqueur. The whole mess was delicious, and broke our training and loosened our tongues—especially Coop's.

Lainie raised her second or third glass of wine and said, "Here's to Father Madden."

"Damn it," Coop protested, "I won't drink to that. He's too good for that crap."

"The priesthood? Crap?" said Lainie.

"If it pulls him out of boxin'," Coop said intensely. "Listen, I talk about turning pro, and I will. But he's got the best damn right hand, and the moves, and the pure guts . . . hell, he could be a champion! You can go ahead and pray, Cully, and go to church. But don't piss it all away! Listen! You ask Wash. He's got a belt on you in four, five years, and he mean it! That old man don't fart around with maybes!"

Coop had gotten a bit loud and Lainie put a hand on his arm. She turned to me. "Cully, do you really like boxing?"

"Not as much as Coop does. And, hell Coop, you're going to be the champion, not me."

"Bullshit!"

"You will, Coop, and if you don't know it, let me tell you." I had to hold up a hand to silence him. "Let me get this said. You're the tiger. I'm the guy who fights the tiger. You fight, kill, move on. I fight, kill, and worry about what I just did." I paused for breath, and Coop let me hold the floor. "You remember Girardeau? Crazy Dixon? I took his heart. And I kept thinking about Blake's poem: 'Tyger! Tyger! burning bright in the forests of the night.' Crazy isn't burning bright any more, Coop. And I did that. And I'm not proud of it." I leaned to him. "You be champion, Coop. I just haven't got the belly for it."

Coop looked at me steadily for a long moment, then shook his head. "Okay, Cully. You be a priest. But it's a goddamn shame."

We managed to get out of there without further argument. Coop went home with Lainie, and I walked down to Canal to get the streetcar for the Garden District. The doors of the nightclubs were open all along Bourbon Street, and I'd never seen anything like it. Or heard anything like it. The near-naked girls were swinging on their poles, the bands were brassing out the jazz and the blues and New Orleans ragtime, and the streets were teaming with more varieties of humanity than I'd imagined existed. Homosexuals with big round patches cut out of the ass of their pants—apparently to offer their buttocks to the world—and women dressed in bright orange or yellow or red dresses hanging out on the doorsteps displaying their bodies so flagrantly that I was embarrassed for them. And they would say, "Come on, soldier. Dip your big wick," and I would shrivel at the heart, thinking: Dear God, how has it come to this? How in hell did we fall this far?

And at the same time I knew I was being a prudish horse's ass, a perfectly formed product of my mother's sexual hangups. So I tried to pray it from both sides, and got on the streetcar thinking that I'd damned well better get me to a monastery, or I'd soon be a depraved wretch running along Bourbon Street with my tongue hanging out.

I got up early and went to mass at St. Louis Cathedral, and received communion. I wasn't sure I was in a state of grace, but I've always thought if the thing wasn't right up there staring at me, it probably wasn't a mortal sin. There was a group of black nuns in attendance, all wearing the same habit. I asked an usher who they were, and he looked surprised, and said: "They are the Sisters of the Holy Family. Everybody knows the sisters." I had never seen a black nun before, and I was both amazed and edified. Having some small idea of what Southern blacks have to put up with, I saluted them for taking the potential for opprobrium a step further by putting on a Roman Catholic habit. Such women were heroes and ought to get the congressional Medal of Honor.

Which gives you an idea of how pompous and pietistic I could get when in a religious mode.

We had a late breakfast—steak again, of course—and got interrupted by Lieutenant March. He said that he had to be running: he had gotten a call from the colonel, who had a special assignment for him. I looked at Wash. He looked back and gave me a small nod. Wash had gotten through to the colonel. I felt like standing up and leading a team cheer. March said something about us doing well against the Marines, and then said: "And I certainly hope your general conduct has benefited from my presence." Coop started to laugh, covered his mouth, but the fuse was lighted. We were all staring down into our plates, suppressing as best we could, when Lieutenant March threw us a salute and fell away toward the front desk trying to look military.

We checked out without incident and went over to Wash's hotel, which turned out to be on North Rampart Street instead of Basin. It wasn't much, but it was clean and had a courtyard with a three-piece rooty-toot band—a tap drum, a cornet, and a guitar. They played throughout brunch and ruined our attempts to grab a midday nap. When they played "Just a Closer Walk with Thee," I was put to wondering who I'd rather have a closer walk with: God or Cornelia. At the moment, Cornelia was running slightly ahead.

EIGHTEEN

I'm standin' at the crossroad, babe
I believe I'm sinkin' down.

Robert Johnson, "Cross Road Blues"

We drove down to the wharf and found the steamboat tied up at the foot of Canal Street. It was decorated like a birthday cake, with pennants and flags and banners. There was a big banner that read, "An Afternoon of Exhibition Boxing."

"She-it," Wash said. "The mob think they're fooling anybody?"

The ring was on the upper rear deck, oversized and underpadded, with colored streamers tied to the ropes. There were folding chairs on all four sides, and already a sizable crowd in place, almost all white, dressed in white, and shining white in the sun.

We found Tookie Snodgrass talking unctuously to a group of women. He broke away when he saw Wash, came over.

"The money's okay, Wash. You only lose a thousand."

"I get it back with the bonus."

"What bonus?"

"We fightin' the semi-main and the main. We win both, we get a thousand bonus. And don't tell me you forgot."

"Oh, right. Of course. But your boys got to really take 'em out."

"Don't you worry about that," Wash said. "They be down, out, and sincerely starched."

There was a common dressing room, and they had already started taping the opponents. Wash rushed over, inspected what was going on, demanded two wraps over gauze be removed.

"We taping to the skin, gentlemen," Wash said. "Directly to the skin, and no damn arguments."

There was an argument, and it was finally decided that the three who would be fighting us would tape to the skin, and the others could tape any way they damn well pleased. I noticed that two of our opponents were white—and, sure as hell, they were up against Coop and me. Beefy looking, both of them, and overweight, but they looked mean enough, and I braced myself for an interesting afternoon.

We stretched out on benches in the passenger cabin until we got the call. When they came for Waldo, I went up with him to help Wash and Ace with the water bucket. Waldo's man was one of the Algiers boys, a dedicated clown who probably went on to a big career in vaudeville. He danced, he ducked, he ran in circles. Waldo finally caught up with him in the second round and tagged him nicely. He went down, played dead for a moment, then got up and did a forward somersault to his feet as the bell rang.

Waldo came back to the corner. "Jesus, Boss, I know this is a exhibition, but this is ridiculous."

"Lean on him," Wash said. "He'll go quiet."

"Do I have to take him out?"

"If you got any mercy."

Waldo went out and had mercy. The clown started dancing in and butting. Waldo took two of these, then, at the propitious moment looked out at the crowd as if to ask an *indulto*, but the crowd hollered, "Pound him!" Waldo, holding him off with his left, measured him with the right and dropped him. The crowd cheered.

"So much for goddamn exhibition," Wash said.

Spider Webb had taken one of the cars to pick up Cornelia, and they arrived just as I was about to go on. Spider shouted my name, and when I spotted him he was standing behind Cornelia and Prissy, pointing vigorously. I waved my thanks, and waved again to Cornelia, who twinkled her fingers at me and smiled. I was ready to face suet man.

He was sturdy enough and willing, but he had absolutely no science. He was very busy with footwork: he would do a little shag, throw two or three punches short, and dance out again. I figured I'd have to wait him out, catch him the middle of his shag, and drop one in. Well, it took awhile. At the end of the second round, Wash said, "You enjoyin' the cotillion?"

"Wash, he hasn't won a point."

"You want us to get the goddamned bonus?"

"Yeah."

"Put him down."

I finally got him going left when he should have gone right, and stuck a right on his nose. He went down, apparently thought about getting up, noted the flowing blood, and did a theatrical collapse.

I went over to Wash. "I wonder what the hell he thinks he's doing in the ring."

"Never mind that. Look at Cornelia."

I looked, and there she was on her feet, applauding firmly. And she looked beautiful and happy and so gorgeous in white that I wanted to go to her and gather her up. But the manly art frowns on such displays, so I hung in the corner to work Coop's fight.

When Coop came up, I pointed out his opponent, whom we were told went by the name of Lyle Beaudine. He was off to one side getting massaged with oil by two handlers.

"Wash," Coop said. "Is that shit legal?"

"I'm goin' to check it out," Wash said. He came back grimacing. "They say it sun oil, keep him from burnin' his white ass."

"Well, he white as a ripe pig," Coop said. "We get him out of the sun right quick." Coop turned to me. "These people serious, Cully?"

"Not so far. But Beaudine looks like he's gone a few rounds."

"Lainie here?"

I looked over and there she was, apparently in the process of being introduced to Cornelia and Prissy. I pointed. "Over there, with Cornelia."

Coop stood up and waved, and I joined him, and they all waved back vigorously. God, I thought, this is no way to encourage vocations.

Beaudine came out munching on his mouthpiece, thrusting out his chin, looking ludicrously confident, even nodding at the spectators as if they were his personal guests and he was going to entertain them. An amiable man, assured of his presence and welcome. Then Coop stuck him with two brisk left jabs, and the facade, as they say, fell away. He issued something like a growl and came boring in. His head was moving in vicious chops, his elbows were constantly firing, and he proceeded to go into one bull charge after another, using the clinches to rub with his laces and butt with his head. Coop did his best to keep him off, uppercutting and hooking, but it was clear that Beaudine could take a very good punch. And very clear that he was the foulest son-of-a-bitch yet seen, thumbing, rabbit punching, and holding and hitting. He probably had ten, twelve pounds on Coop and used every ounce of it.

Coop's eye came open within the first minute, and he came back to the corner covered with blood.

"You got to hold him off!" Wash said. "Stick him and move."

"It's like hittin' a steel butterball," Coop said. "He look fat, but he don't give!"

We got the bleeding stopped, and the second round went a little better, with Coop's speed finally settling in. But this was a bully boy for sure, with a jaw like a pine knot. Coop came back after the second round and said, "He's tryin' to knee me!"

"I know," Wash said. "Knee him back."

"I already got warned by the goddamned referee."

"Don't worry about him. He bought and paid for. Just do what got to be done."

Coop went out for the third round, Beaudine came in swinging rights and lefts at the body, and the third or fourth punch caught Coop full in the cup. I heard Coop cry out in pain. What happened next defies belief. With Coop bent over, clutching at his balls, Beaudine walked right in, took Coop's head under his right elbow—chicken-winging they call it—and ran the top of Coop's head into the unpadded ring post.

It sounded like a coconut hit with a metal bat. Coop fell straight down on his face, and lay still except for the reflexive kicking of his legs. Beaudine turned and sprinted for his corner. Wash almost caught him, but Beaudine's handlers got him out of the ring and ran him to cover. The referee declared Coop the winner by reason of flagrant foul, and the spectators went into a steady uproar—pro and con, as I made it out. Running people into ring posts was apparently a semi-respectable ring tactic. In Louisiana.

They brought up an ambulance, we put him on a stretcher, and I could see a long split across the top of his head, the blood oozing out. Lainie came running, but they kept her away. The doctor told her Coop was fine, still alive. They also tried to keep Wash and me off, but we shoved our way into the ambulance with the ring doctor. My last vision of the wharf was of Cornelia, standing with Lainie, tears streaming down her lovely face.

Some exhibition.

The ring doctor and an assistant put some rough stitches in the head wound, and dressed it. Then the doctor sat back and said: "Jesus, I hope he doesn't die on my watch."

I looked at Wash. "Shall we throw him out the back door?"

Wash shook his head. "White trash," he said softly. "Don't want to litter the street."

NINETEEN

I believe . . .
I believe my time ain't long.

Robert Johnson, "Ramblin' On My Mind" (take 2)

The hospital was Catholic, and the nun across the counter looked at me sternly. "What is his religious preference?" she said.

"Black," I said.

Wash poked me with his elbow. "Catholic," he said. "Roman Catholic."

They took Coop directly into an operating room. Wash and I waited outside until a doctor came out and said that Coop was in coma, and that it was very difficult at this stage to determine the seriousness of the injury. But they were working on it. Then the doctor went back inside. The nun came over to ask about next of kin, and neither Wash nor I could help her. I was about to give her Lainie's name and business address when Lainie came in, alone.

"How is he?" she asked.

I told her what the doctor had said. "I think he just got knocked out."

"Pray God," she said.

Which emboldened the nun to ask if Lainie were next of kin. "Well, I'm about as close as you'll get," Lainie said. And the nun led Lainie over to the counter to sign something.

Wash stood up. "You hold the fort, Cully. I got to go down and see Tookie Snodgrass about some money."

Then the team came in. They had gone back to the hotel and gotten a toothbrush and other things for Coop. The nun took them and put them in a plastic bag, and marked it. And we all sat around and looked at the floor until Wash came in.

"Smart bastards," he said.

"You got the money?"

"Oh sure. But they already charged Beaudine with battery or somethin', got him up before a magistrate where he pled guilty and got a fifty dollar fine. He's clear. They covered their asses."

"You believe them?"

"Why not? They wasn't a whole hell of a lot we could have done anyways. Not in this town."

I knew he was right. Injury in boxing is almost never a cause of action. When you get in the ring, you take your death with you. If you've still got it on the hip when you come out, you win. Even if you lose. But I had it in mind that, if Coop should not come out of that coma, Mr. Beaudine would not get away with that fifty dollar fine. If I had to waylay the son-of-a-bitch.

Lainie had work to do—a "prospect"—and, after my reassurances that Coop would come out of it fine, she asked Ace for a ride to her office. The whole team volunteered. She told me that Cornelia and Prissy had had to get back to the school, but that Lainie had given her the name of the hospital. Chappie said they'd go eat afterward, so Wash gave Sonny some money, and they trooped out, looking worried but saying that nobody could really hurt Coop.

Wash and I sat there for an hour, mostly in silence, until they came out and said that they had closed the wounds, that there was no apparent skull fracture, that Coop's life signs were reasonably stable, and that he was being moved to intensive care, condition critical. We would not be allowed to see him that evening.

When they left—two lugubrious doctors and a nurse—Wash turned to me. "Is that good news?"

"Only one way it could be worse."

Wash nodded. "Goddamn. We should've just gone down and fought the Marines. I shouldn't have got us into this shit."

"Don't blame yourself, Wash. Without the river fights, the Marines would just walk us over. You know that."

"You think Coop's going to make it?"

"Yeah, I do. He's a tough man."

Wash nodded. "You goin' to let me buy you some dinner?"

"No, thanks. I'm not hungry. You go ahead. I'll call the hotel if there's any news."

"Okay, Cully. Here's twenty for cab fare and food, when you get around to it." He stood there looking down at me. Then he rested his hand on my shoulder for a moment, turned, and went out.

I went down to the hospital chapel. The red sacristy lamp was the only light, and I prayed there for most of an hour.

What I had to take up with God was whether He was somehow complicit in the problem of evil. Things like this shouldn't happen. So why do they? Has God somehow involved Himself in the playing out of a dualist morality play? One in which He is as involved in evil as we are? Is God playing with us, and with all being, good and evil? Is He working it out for Himself, still in the process of becoming Himself, while we dance the jig between heaven and hell? But if this were so, does He also suffer, and does He take the risk with us? Is He taking that risk of failing day by day, as we do? Could we lose the whole god-damned shooting match to the forces of evil? Did Jesus Christ, the Son, come to earth to help the Father out? Save the Father's bacon by justifying His creation? But if the beast has a fair chance of winning, shouldn't somebody let us know? So we can gird up our loins and make a better fight of it? Is the silence of God on these questions justifiable? Is the silence of God going to weave our winding sheet? Speak, God, so we can hear.

"De profundis clamavi ad te Domine. Domine ad adjuvandam me festina," I prayed, remembering some of my altar boy Latin.

And, at last, I prayed: "Dear God, I ask that you bring Coop out of it and restore him to health. This is certainly within Your power, and I ask it most solemnly in the name of Your Beloved Son, Jesus Christ our Lord. Amen."

Then I went out, heavy at heart, listening to the silence.

Coop's condition hadn't changed the next morning, and we were still not allowed to see him. Wash called a meeting and said he didn't want us working out at the New Orleans Boxing Club. Could lead to murder. So he had called out to Biloxi to see if there were gym facilities available. There were. And he had found a good, cheap hotel for us, and he suggested we leave within the hour. "They's not a damned thing we can do for Coop," he said. "Except win a few fights for him. Sittin' around here on our funk ain't goin' to help anybody. So, pack it up, an' let's get on the road."

We stopped in Bay St. Louis to eat, and I called the hospital. Coop's condition had been changed to extremely critical. I demanded to speak to a doctor, and he said there was now fluid on the brain, and then went on with the usual bullshit: "But he's young, in excellent general health, and we are cautiously optimistic."

Yeah. Right. Then the doctor added that they had given him the last rites.

I went back to the table and didn't say anything, but Wash read me.

"Worse?" he said.

"Last rites," I said.

Wash bowed his head.

⌞⌝⌞⌝⌞⌝

Something had been working on me, a deep grief and a deeper anger, and when were back on the road, I finally got it out and into words.

"Wash?"

"Yeah."

"You still talking to Tookie Snodgrass?"

"Well, I did hit him a short shot, but if I talk he'll listen."

"Good. I want to fight Beaudine."

Wash heaved a moaning sigh. "You do?"

"I do. And I can lick the bastard."

"He got pounds on you, Cully. Twenty, twenty-five of 'em. Sure, I can arrange it. But he hit you in the balls, first crack out of the box."

"No, he won't. I've been thinking about it. I'll fend him off and work his arms, like the Cuban did to me. Then, when he can't lift them, I'll take his goddamned head off."

Wash looked at me, eyebrows raised. "That one I would *pay*

to see." He smiled a small smile, shook his head. "Who-ee she-it! And Old Tookie, he goin' to pay a big fat waddy just to get through the door!"

"What do you guys think?"

"Love it!" Chappie said. "But I should fight him."

"He'd never take you on. You outweigh him."

Chappie nodded, then broke out in a big grin. "I got me a new verse!"

And he sang it for us.

"Cully Madden flams and flims, got us runnin' on our rims. Jesus, woman, cain't you see? You have had your piece of me!"

We all laughed, and, for the first time, I realized that the woman of Chappie's song had to be boxing.

TWENTY

She's a kind-hearted mama
She studies evil all the time . . .
You well's to kill me, baby
As to have it on your mind.

Robert Johnson, "Kind Hearted Woman Blues" (take 2)

Wash's hotel in Biloxi was over by one of the shrimp canneries, and the stink was awful. But the air conditioning worked, and it was close to the boxing gym, which was down near the seawall. Wash explained to us that we could stay over on Keesler Field with the rest of the teams, but we agreed with his choice. It cost us a little money, but we didn't really want to mix with the Marines until we stepped into the ring with them. And any time we could avoid military chow, we avoided it, especially since they were offering no training table amenities at Keesler.

The owner of the gym was a big man with a rumbling bass voice and the beat-up eyes of a long-time opponent. But a lovely man, with a world-encompassing smile and the grace and manners of a prince of the realm. He was probably the blackest man I have ever seen, and he would say: "They got to me early on, when the ink was fresh out of the gourd." His name was Elijah "Lige" Pickering, and he gathered us all in unto him, including Wash, as if we were a bunch of motherless children. Which, of course, at the time, we were.

We worked out morning and afternoon and ate lunch at a soul food joint that served a chicken-fried steak that was at least sinful. I had it for lunch and dinner and, since I was trying to take on weight, added mashed potatoes and gravy and Shreveport pie for dessert. After three days of this, I was up to one-sixty-six, and still hard as a rock. Wash told me to be careful because the AAU was going to supervise the weigh-ins, but I figured I could boil it down after a long morning in the steambath.

I called the hospital twice a day; no change in Coop. Still in deep coma. I called Miss Chamberlin's several times, and finally got through once to Cornelia. She said she had been praying nonstop for him and was going to try to get in to see him. She wished me luck against the Marines. And she said she missed me. I said I missed her, and I did, and I left the phone booth light-headed, full of noble thoughts of romantic love.

We got word Wednesday night that we would be up Thursday and Friday. Bantam, feather, light welter, junior middle on Thursday, the rest on Friday. With Coop gone, we went in with a forfeit. The Marines had a slight weight variance at middleweight; their man was one-sixty-four and didn't figure to get it down any further. Wash and I laughed. "God smilin' on you, Cully. You and that chicken-fried steak."

Wash finally ironed out the deal with Tookie Snodgrass on Wednesday night for a Saturday fight. We would get a thousand dollars. I'd be the only member of the team fighting. Beaudine promised to come in at one eighty, and we would be billed as a special added attraction by the New Orleans Boxing Club. "He read me the ad," Wash said. "He's billin' it as a grudge fight."

"Well, he's got that right."

"Now, Cully, you sure? I mean you fightin' Friday, and that Marine could be a bear."

"Wash, I don't care if he's King Kong. I want it just the way we've got it. Let's just pray that Beaudine shows up."

Wash looked at me, chuckled. "Goddamn. You the real article."

Lige Pickering worked two rounds with me on Wednesday, and I told him about Beaudine. He said: "Sure, go for the arms, but do not neglect the lung shots. Short shots, turning your feet as you throw. And don't forget the little twist of the wrist as the punch lands." He showed me, and I remembered my father had shown me. But I'd forgotten. "You ever want to break a nose, the little twist will do it ever' time." I practiced it, and when Wash came in he just stood in the back of the gym and watched. Later on, he said, "You got a little tip on the twist, did ya'?"

"Yeah," I said.

"Good," Wash said. "But use it very careful. Or you could break your damn arm."

⌞⌝⌞⌝⌞⌝

We went over to Keesler on Thursday morning and checked in at the gym. The AAU was running the show, but the weigh-ins were nothing special, and Spider was very annoyed that he'd spent half the night in the steam bath getting down to weight.

Spider led off, of course, and taught his opponent quite a few things about the sweet science. I don't think he laid a glove on Spider the entire first round. I was working the corner, and I asked Spider how he was doing it. Spider said: "I don't know. This cat was made for me. He come in a box with my name on it."

Spider was an expert at point-fighting, which the AAU loved to see, and the Marine didn't win a round. The Marine manager, Sergeant Cutler, was damned near apoplectic. The Marines had obviously come with the intention of winning every fight. But fight one was no contest.

"He's a ringer!" Cutler shouted. "He's a goddamned ringer."

Wash grinned. "He keep that up, I'll go over and ring him."

Stone drew a man who had obviously been in the Corps since Tripoli. A leatherneck, and a leather jaw. In the first thirty seconds, he had Stone out on his feet. But Stone hung in, and came back to the corner on his heels. Wash lit into him. "Goddamn, boy, you playin' heavy bag? No never mind, because you already took all he's got. So, this ain't goin' two rounds, 'cause it's your turn. Now go out there and *take him out!*"

Stone looked dubious, but gathered himself and had at it. The Marine looked startled as he took Stone's first left hook. And he looked dead when they counted him out.

"Way to go, Stone," I said.

"I got to go throw up," Stone said. "I think he broke my throat." He threw up in the bucket, and I had to take it in and dump it. But that was two, and the Marines were getting truly pissed off.

Sonny was across the ring and into his man's face before he was fully off the stool. Cutler cried foul, whereupon Sonny waded in. The Marine never got out of his corner. Sonny moved from one side to the other, throwing his weight with every shot. The Marine was counted out in forty-five seconds of the first round.

"What the hell is this?" shouted Sergeant Cutler. "Goddamn Air Force hired them a team of pros!"

"I really may have to go over and tap him one," Wash said. "But we'll wait till after the waltz."

Waldo lucked out. His man was older, thick in the middle, eyes surrounded with cut scars. He'd been in the Marines since Montezuma. Waldo placed four shots on the liver and the old man was almost bent double. Still, he could hit, and caught Waldo with a hook near the end of the first round that almost ended the affair. We got Waldo up with the salts and the cold iron, and he went out and fought a businesslike second round. Early in the third round, the Marine decided to launch a proper offensive. It lasted two swings. Then Waldo caught him coming in with a perfect uppercut, and the bout was over. The Marine stood for a moment, looking astonished, then danced in a small circle, and fell down. Waldo came over to the corner, grinning. "Coop taught me that shot," he said. "Elbow in tight, lift off the right toes."

"You're a goddamn killer, Waldo," Wash said. "And God bless Coop."

We didn't get out of there without a verbal assault from Sergeant Cutler, about an AAU and intra-service investigation. Wash listened a minute, then said, "Listen, you horse's ass, you want to settle this like a real man, put on the gloves, get in the ring. I teach you some Air Force manners."

Sergeant Cutler wasn't having any. It well may have been the most judicious decision of his military life.

TWENTY-ONE

Early this mornin'
when you knocked upon my door . . .
And I said, "Hello, Satan,
I believe it's time to go.

Robert Johnson, "Me And The Devil Blues"

I got through to Cornelia that evening, and she had been to see Coop.

"He's still in coma?"

"Yes, but he comes in and out. He recognized me, called me by name. But then he was gone again."

"It's very good of you to go see him."

"I went with Lainie. We have become friends."

"What's Miss Chamberlin say about it?"

"We had words, but she finally gave her blessing. She called the hospital to make sure that I was there. She's not a very trusting person. Occupational hazard, I guess."

"What did you tell her?"

"I told her we have an obligation to visit the sick."

I shook my head. Cornelia was something else. "Well, I appreciate it, and I'm certain Coop does."

"He doesn't look well at all, Cully. I hope you can come back soon."

"We'll be heading back right after the fights tomorrow. We should be there by early evening. I'll give you a call."

"I'll be waiting. Maybe I can go to the hospital with you."

"Let's do it. I'll come for you in one of the cars."

"Thank you, Cully. I look forward to it."

I hung up thinking that things were moving a little too quickly here, between Cornelia and me, and that I'd better find a way to put on the brakes. I was still very serious about the priesthood, but at times it was beginning to look like just another option. Was it what I really wanted? Not while I was looking at Cornelia it wasn't. But, with Coop down, I really couldn't address it properly. I just said a "Hail, Holy Queen" and let it slide.

How Chappie persuaded Wash that we ought to go out that night I'll never know. Wash's strict rule was that we be in bed by 10 P.M. on a night before a fight, and no exceptions. But Chappie had somewhere heard (probably from Lige Pickering) that there was something happening out on the Gulfport road that was truly worth our while. So Wash relented.

We had the required steak dinner at a Creole French restaurant. Pepper steak that I was sure did extensive damage to the roof of my mouth.

Then, guided by Chappie, we went out to a clapboard shack jazz joint on the Gulfport Road. The performer was a young black man in his late twenties or early thirties, whose name, as I recall, was Tyler. He was doing a singing tribute to Blind Willie Johnson, accompanying himself on the guitar.

And somewhere near the beginning he spoke to the audience. "I was born blind. But Willie Johnson was blinded by his stepmother when he was seven. She was mad because Willie's father had beaten her when he found her with another man. Willie Johnson's first guitar was made out of a cigar box, and he become a singer. But before that woman threw lye in his face, what he wanted to be was a preacher. You listen to his songs, you hear the preacher, and you hear the black man cryin' out to his Lord."

He started with "I Know His Blood Can Make Me Whole," done mostly in a harsh, grating growl that came smashing into your face like a bucket of stones. Then he did "Mother's Children Have a Hard Time," "Lord I Can't Just Keep from Crying," "Trouble Will Soon Be Over," and ended the first set with "Dark Was the Night—Cold Was the Ground"—a primitive roar—and with a sweet-voiced rendition of "Jesus Make Up My Dying Bed." The applause went on for two minutes, and I sat there stunned, an emotional basket case. The black soul had been ripped out of its body and held aloft, and by God I let the tears run down my white face, thinking of Coop.

Wash got us up and out, and I don't think I said a word all the way back to the hotel. Wash saw me to the door of my room. "You let it all out tomorrow, Cully. You be fine."

I nodded and closed the door, but I knew what I was feeling had nothing to do with tomorrow's Marine. It had to do with Lyle Beaudine, and by the time I went to sleep, I had got it surrounded and corked for later release.

TWENTY-TWO

Let your light from the lighthouse,
Shine on me.

Blind Willie Johnson, "Let Your Light Shine on Me"

Mose was finally in a fighting mood and took his man on the rise. Which is to say that the Marine came out sort of hopping, moving frenetically, trying to punch down on Mose. Well, at the start of one of his hops, Mose caught him going up, moved in, and tapped his descending chin with a sturdy uppercut. The Marine toppled over backward and fell hard. He got up, but the damage was done, and Mose simply banged him around the ring for three rounds. Decision to Mose, and no comment from the Marine corner.

I ran into a buzzsaw—blond, blue-eyed, with the intensity of a gunfighter. Between rounds, Wash ragged me that I wasn't seeing to business, but I was; I just couldn't rouse very much interest in the proceeding. He was a "pointer," but he was nowhere near hurting me, and I just did enough to keep him engaged and honest. I caught a lot of punches and threw a few, including one that knocked him to one knee in the third round, but it was a generally friendly exercise in what I call pepper-pot boxing. Lots of pop-and-run, cunning moves, and nobody gets hurt. They called it a draw, although I really thought the Marine's sheer expenditure of energy had earned him a win.

Wash tried to be sarcastic. "I certainly hope you managed to save somethin' for Beaudine after that terrible ordeal."

"Oh, I don't know, Wash. Just watching him was an awful strain on the eyeballs."

"Right. A strain on balls all around."

Chappie's fight was a bloodbath on both sides. The Marine was bigger and a fair match for Chappie in slugging power and verve. He was a fine physical specimen, had knocked out his last nineteen opponents, was Navy Fleet champion or some such, and was supposed to be an excellent pro prospect. Chappie wasn't buying any. He came in with the body attack, drove four shots to the lungs and liver, delivered a fine accidental butt, and had the Marine back on the ropes, covering, before the fight was ten seconds old. But the Marine fought back with a beautiful jab, bicycled his way out of trouble, and the fight settled into a battle of attrition. Each bloodied the other very quickly, and just as quickly they decided to slug it out at center ring. It looked like Dempsey/Firpo, with sweat and blood filling the air around their heads.

I had no doubt of the outcome. Chappie could hit like a Sherman tank, and I figured it was only a matter of time before he made just the right connection. It came with fourteen seconds left in the first round. He caught the Marine with a right cross, standing flat-footed in front of him, all his power flowing from the heels as he turned his ass into the punch. A splat like a shovel on mud, and the Marine went sliding along the ropes and into his corner, where he fell with a broken jaw.

Chappie came back to the corner in serious need of repair,

but he was grinning, and he said, "Damn, I wish Coop had been here to see that punch."

The Air Force had one forfeit, one draw, and six wins, and so we were in the top position for the service semifinals. We went back to the hotel pounding the roofs of the cars and singing "Into the air junior birdmen!"

It was a very good time, and I tried to ride the high and meet the mood. But as soon as we'd gotten Chappie sewed up, I asked that we leave at once for New Orleans, and Wash, to his credit, said sure, and issued the marching orders.

One last note: Marine Sergeant Cutler filed a protest and called for an investigation of the Air Force boxing team. I hope he got all the facts and found out that he'd been trashed by what was probably the most unkempt, underprivileged, underfunded bunch of itinerant streetfighters ever to represent a U.S. military service.

TWENTY-THREE

I have a Bible in my home,
I don't read, my soul be lost.
Nobody's fault but mine.

Blind Willie Johnson,
"It's Nobody's Fault but Mine"

Miss Chamberlin had decided enough was enough, and would not allow Cornelia to accompany me to the hospital.

"I have my responsibilities," she said to me belligerently.

"Yes, ma'am."

"My girls are in my absolute care."

"Yes, ma'am."

"I understand your friend is a Niggra, and he's in a charity ward of Charity Hospital."

"Yes, ma'm."

"Well, that is a dangerous place for a young white girl."

"Well, ma'am, I understand your position completely. But I must disagree with it. This man is my friend, and he is in mortal danger, and we do have an obligation to visit the sick."

"Don't you preach to me, young man! I've had all I can stomach from Cornelia! We have an obligation to visit *our* sick! Not just any old body's sick!"

"Yes, ma'am. An excellent Protestant distinction, I'm sure, but sick is sick."

"Don't you bandy words with me, young man! I know your true motives, and the answer is no!"

"Yes, ma'am."

When I got out to the car, Tremaine, who was driving said, "No need to translate. I could hear her all the way out here."

"Old goddamn dreadnought."

"Yeah, but you know, Cully, I'd put my kids with her anytime."

"I suppose so."

"'Cause a black ward *is* a dangerous place."

"Let's go see Coop."

I went into Coop's room. There were three other intensive care patients in other beds, but the main light was over Coop's bed.

"The young lady was here most of last night," the nurse said.

"Lainie?"

"I think that's her name."

"Were they able to speak?"

"He said a few words. You've got five minutes."

I went over to Coop. After a moment, I reached down and touched his hand. His eyes flickered open. But no focus.

"I know you probably can't hear me, Coop. But we starched the Marines." No reaction. "I committed the only draw. But the other guys—especially Chappie—you should have seen them."

Still no visible reaction.

"I'll be back, Coop. They're throwing me out. One thing. Wash has fixed me up with Beaudine. Tomorrow night." Coop's hand closed on mine. "I mean to do him damage, Coop. I mean to leave marks on him."

Coop's hand tightened on mine, held tight, then released. His eyes closed. But I knew he had heard.

I backed out of the room, my eyes on Coop.

"Hey, Coop," I said. "Hang easy. You're walking out of here. No damn way you're not walking out of here."

I ran into Lainie outside the chapel, and she immediately began to cry. I took her in my arms and held her, and felt myself growing older. And very, very tired. When Lainie had gone up for her time with Coop, I went back to the hotel and got into bed feeling like a dead man. And I slept like one.

TWENTY-FOUR

Motherless children have a hard time
Mother's dead
Well don't have anywhere to go,
Wandering 'round from door to door . . .
Have a hard time . . .

Blind Willie Johnson,
"Motherless Children Have a Hard Time"

The New Orleans Boxing Club was stuffed to the spandrels by fight time Saturday night. Tookie Snodgrass had gotten the word out for sure, and the blood was up and the faithful all in attendance. Wash and Ace and I got to the back entrance a full hour before we were up, but there were ten bouts altogether, and we had to share a rat-trap dressing room with four other fighters. Fortunately, Beaudine was not one of them. When the other fighters found out who I was, they immediately began to show deference and to make room: I was the other half of Lyle Beaudine's grudge fight, and was therefore an instant celebrity.

"What is this, Wash? Is the son-of-a-bitch that well known?"

"He is now," Wash said. "He the big bad boy."

Wash went over to see to Beaudine's taping and brought Tookie back to see to mine. Tookie was clearly very excited.

"Haven't had a crowd like this since Lee Scammon," he said.

"Who in the hell is Lee Scammon?" Wash said.

"You don't know?"

"No, and don't tell me," Wash said. "Is your boy goin' to behave hisself tonight?"

"Lyle?" Tookie said. "Oh, Lord yes. He had his lesson."

"No, he ain't," Wash said. "But he goin' to get it."

"Well, best of luck."

"Never mind best of luck. Five hundred now."

"Oh, right."

Tookie counted out five hundred on the rubbing table. Wash picked it up. "I see you first thing this is over," Wash said. "If I don't, you'll wish I had."

"Oh, I'll be here," Tookie said. "To tell you maybe next time." He grinned a pallid little grin and went out.

"I think," Wash said, "they's worse trash in this world, but I ain't yet met up with it. Thank God."

They were forty minutes off schedule when we got the call. I was damned near asleep on the table, but I felt fine. Wash put me through a five-minute warm up, then said: "They asked if we could skip the headgear. I said yes. Okay with you?"

"Sure. But the AAU—"

"The AAU ain't goin' to be anywhere near this," Wash said.

"Smile, Wash," I said. "It's just a goddamn fight."

He embraced me. "You do me proud, Cully. You do Coop proud."

By the time we got into the ring, I wished I were back in East Saint. It was the most raucous, hostile, mean-spirited crowd since God invented vituperation. When I simply looked out toward the first couple of rows, a mighty boo erupted. Ace, who enjoyed such things, smiled at me and shouted, "Oh, ain't we got a dandy!"

More uproar when Beaudine entered the ring. I had an advantage on him because I'd seen him fight but he hadn't seen me fight. Yet that looked like the only advantage because he had beefed himself up big time; he had to weigh one-ninety-five or better.

"Wash," I shouted. "Look at him!"

"I know, I know!" Wash shouted back. "But the fight is on! You didn't want to call it off?"

"Hell no! But I may need an ax!"

In the center of the ring, the referee mumbled and Beaudine glowered. I studied him with some curiosity. He truly did look like a boar hog, with his pricky little eyes and his turned-up snout. We will slaughter the fatted pig, I thought, and we will serve him up with an apple in his mouth.

Beaudine came out of his corner at the bell with truly surprising speed. He was upon me before I could cover, swung a short right, and knocked me down. I watched him dance away to a neutral corner, and I thought, My God, where are my legs? He's taken my legs. Wash, not three feet from me, was howling, "If you hurt, stay down!"

"Right," I said. Then I found my legs, and used the ropes to get up as the man counted seven. I said to myself: Cully, can the whimsy and other bullshit. It's time to kill.

He came out fast as I moved toward him. I circled to his left and socked a right hook deep in his fatty side. Then, as he lurched, followed with another hook to the jaw. And he went down. I couldn't bloody believe it, and neither could he. As I got to the neutral corner, he looked around at me as if to ask, as others had done, What the hell was that? That, I said to myself, is the coming of the Lord. And you ain't seen nothing yet.

He came at me more cautiously, and I let him come. And now I started working his arms. He had a sort of cross-armed defense, and liked to backhand out of it. I made him pay every time he uncrossed by jabs to the face, and when he crossed his arms again, I pounded on them. The jabs soon opened an eye cut, and then another cut below the first. He tried ducking low and throwing to my gut, but I danced away and brought the uppercut when I could. He had slowed down drastically, and was breathing heavily, and lost his mouthpiece just as the first round ended.

"You ain't layin' it on him, Cully," Wash said.

"I'm getting to it," I said.

"He's still got the power," Wash said. "Don't slight him."

I didn't. I just kept working the arms and covering. The arms were coming down, and, in mid-round, I started going to the head. Nothing full bore, but with the twist-snap that Lige Pickering had shown me. I opened both cuts on the one eye and another over his other eye. Then, as he began to flag again, I picked up the pace, drove him back into a corner, and let the right hand go. And I could see his eyes, and I knew that I had him, and I threw the overhand right with ass-and-all behind it, and down he went again.

The crowd was howling. He wasn't out, but he seemed reluctant to get up. Finally, with his corner screaming at him, he rolled to the ropes, grabbed them, and pulled himself up. And he waited there for me, his shoulder half-turned. He was ready to go again, but I'd be damned if I'd let him. I pushed a couple of jabs at him, and clinched. He seemed vastly relieved and started to sag again. I pulled him up and shouted in his face: "No, you goddamn tub of guts! You ain't going down yet!" Whereupon he brought his right elbow, caught me full between the eyes, and damned near shut me down. I backed off, showing blood, and cleared my eyes. And at last got down to serious business.

Seeing the blood, he came at me hard, and I met him straight up. He threw two good punches to my left side and tried a left to the crotch. I caught him as he came out of his crouch and hit him with the right so hard that he spun fully around, so that my left, when it hit, had his full weight on it. He went down like a sack of kelp and lay there, spurting blood from his nose. I was very pleased to find out later that I had broken it.

Back in the corner Wash was grinning. "I seen better. But I ain't never seen worse. You may have killed him." The corner was out staunching the flow of blood, but Beaudine wasn't moving. And the crowd was howling full pitch.

I said, "Wash, let's get the hell out of here. My nose needs some work."

The referee, who had forgotten to count, was still at it when we left the ring.

TWENTY-FIVE

I got some warning
Jesus coming soon.

Blind Willie Johnson, "Jesus Is Coming Soon"

I got to the nurses' station just before 11 P.M., and the duty nurse gave me the cold eye. "Out of the question," she said. "And what happened to you?"

"I was in a fight, and I've got to see him."

Another, younger nurse came up smiling. "Well," she said. "What happened to your nose?"

"It ran into an elbow. How's Coop?"

"You'll be pleased to hear he came out of coma about an hour ago."

"He's awake?"

"Yes. He's still very weak."

I looked at the duty nurse. "Can I see him? Five minutes?"

She heaved a small sigh. "Is he up to it?" she asked the other nurse.

"I think so. But don't expect too much."

I was already halfway down the hall to the intensive care ward.

A night light was on by Coop's bed. The bed was surrounded

by screens, and there was some new equipment on both sides. A young doctor was bending over Coop with a stethoscope, and he put his forefinger to his lips as I came up. Coop's eyes were closed, and he looked awful—drained, shriveled.

"Who are you?" whispered the doctor.

"A friend."

"Well, friend, get your ass out of here."

Then Coop spoke. "Lainie?"

"No, no," said the doctor. "Time to sleep."

"I been asleep," Coop said.

"It's me, Coop," I said.

"Hey," he said, and his eyes came open. "That my man?"

"Listen, you," the doctor said. "He's low, very damn low. He could go any time. Now would you get the hell out of here?"

"Cully?" Coop said.

"They're throwing me out, Coop."

"The hell they are!" Coop said, his voice suddenly strong. "You throw them out, y' hear?"

"Out of my way," I said to the doctor.

"Well, it's on your head," he said.

I went over to the bed. "Jesus God, Coop. You had us worried."

He smiled. "Hello, Cully. How's my man?"

"How are you?"

"Oh, I come and go. Story of my life." He smiled gently. Then, "Hey! That girl, Corny?"

"Yes."

"She's one of the good ones, Cully. You marry that girl, y'hear?"

"I hear."

"Do it. Or Lainie'll kick your ass."

"When you marry Lainie."

"Oh no. I mean, I don't know, Cully. I just don't know."

"About Lainie?"

"No. Lainie fine. Just fine." His eyes moved over to mine. "You know that song that Robert Johnson sings? Hello, Satan, I believe it's time to go?"

"I remember it."

"Sure. On the car radio. Sing along."

"The hell with it."

"Okay. You fight Beaudine? Look like he broke your nose."

"I whipped his ass, Coop. I broke *his* nose."

"You put him down?"

"Down and out."

"Good. That make Wash happy. He get his stake money."

His voice was fading badly. "Coop? Maybe I ought to go now. Let you rest."

"No, Cully, you stay. Hand me your hand."

He took my hand and, with surprising strength, lifted it a few inches off the sheets. "My man, Cully. Who did for me with old Beaudine. God bless—"

"Coop?"

"Black comin' up, Cully. Black comin' fast now." He closed his eyes, then opened them fiercely. "Goodbye, Cully Madden. You the best ever was. Fight black, Cully. Always fight black."

His hand fell away from mine, and he convulsed. The doctor leaped forward, hit Coop's chest with both hands. But it was over.

Caldwell Cooper, dear friend and one of God's finest, had passed.

TWENTY-SIX

Yes the blues
Is a lowdown achin' heart disease
Like consumption,
Killing me by degrees.

Robert Johnson, "Preachin' Blues
(Up Jumped The Devil)"

How the hell I got through the next two days I do not know. Apparently, I talked to people in a rational manner, made decisions, made arrangements. But I simply wasn't there.

All I was feeling was a deep and overwhelming anger. Where was my good God now? My good God could go take a hike. And I told Him so, and worse. I told Him I could have put forty monkeys at typewriters and they could have drawn up a better plan for the world in four minutes than He had in seven days. I told Him I wanted no more of His vaunted free will if all it did was give us permission to destroy ourselves. And I told Him that there would be no more talk of the priesthood until He had done something intelligible about the problem of evil in the world.

If you think that you cannot get angry enough to say and mean such things, take my word for it. You can. And mean every word. And if you think you can forget how ridiculous you are being, be assured, you can do that, too. Savage indignation conquers all.

The first order of business was to call Wash. He came on the phone full of sleep and annoyance. "Who the hell is this?"

"It's Cully, Wash. Coop is gone."

"Oh God. Oh Christ. Damn! Goddamn!" Then: "You at the hospital?"

"Yes."

"I be right down."

"Wash?"

"Yeah."

"Phone numbers for Lainie and Cornelia are in my room, in Coop's little red book. Please bring it."

"I will."

"And, Wash. I don't want the damned Air Force burying Coop. We've got to do it."

"Well, all right Cully. But we need a next of kin."

"Lainie. His *sister* Lainie."

A moment of silence. "That oughta work. See you real quick."

From whence all this brilliance proceeded, I am at a loss to say. A higher power was at work. I then called Tree Webb at the hotel. He'd already talked to Wash. In fact, the whole team was up and dressing, intending to come down.

"Sure. Come down, Tree. But I want you to be thinking of an undertaker. And of a graveyard where we can bury Coop."

"I got it. I got both of them."

Somehow, I knew he would. "And Tree, we'll need a brass band—the whole shooting match. A proper New Orleans funeral."

"Oh, well. I know Percy Humphrey. He's the leader of the Eureka Brass Band, the best in the city."

"Great. See you soon, Tree."

Lainie walked in around midnight, fresh off a job, looking so beautiful and serene that I hated to tell her what had happened.

As I started, she interrupted. "I know. The nurses told me. I been getting ready for it, Cully. I knew he didn't have long."

She came to me and I held her for a moment, and she said, "Oh Cully. He knew that we loved him. He took that with him."

Then I told her about Coop's last moments and words, and we both wept a little. I recovered enough to tell her about the funeral plans and how she had to be next of kin. She thought it was a very good idea and pointed out that she and Coop did look an awful lot alike.

Then Wash and Ace and the team arrived. I got Wash, Ace, and Tree to one side and we discussed financial matters. Wash said he had a cash reserve of about two thousand dollars, Tree said it should all only cost about twelve hundred, Ace said he had five hundred he could throw in, and we all concluded that we'd have a first-class New Orleans funeral and parade. Then Lainie and I had to deal with the coroner, who told us the body had to be interred within forty-eight hours, or something like that. But Tree had already talked to him, and everything was in hand.

I don't remember any of this. Wash told me most of it on the way home. He told me that I had reduced the undertaker to tears because he'd tried to rip us off with a five thousand dollar casket, or whatever, and that when Percy Humphrey, the leader of the Eureka Brass Funeral and Half-Fast Marching Band, had told me that he could do it with as few as five musicians, I had said no, the whole damned band. This meant eleven players, including two trumpets, snare drum, bass drum, tenor saxophone, alto saxophone, E-Flat clarinet, two trombones, and a sousaphone. Wash said he was relieved that a twenty-one gun salute wasn't available, or I'd have added that. I would not have. I didn't want the military to have anything to do with it.

And so, on Monday afternoon, after he had "lain in state" all morning at the funeral parlor, we set out for the St. Roch

Cemetery on North Rampart Street (situated roughly between St. Ann and St. Peter Streets) to take Coop to his grave. He would not be buried. In New Orleans, the water table is so high that the dead are laid to rest in crypts (or "New Orleans ovens" as they are called). And Tree had arranged it all: the dancers with umbrellas, the half-fast band, the entire Air Force contingent, Lainie, Cornelia, and maybe a dozen friends we didn't know Coop had until Lainie had rounded them up. On the way out we were reverent. On the way back things loosened up a bit, and a festive mood took over. The band was magnificent, and they played "Just a Closer Walk with Thee," "West Lawn Dirge," "Sing On," "Garland of Flowers," "You Tell Me Your Dream," "Lady Be Good," and, of course, "When the Saints Go Marching In," "Didn't He Ramble," and "Amazing Grace." I walked beside the casket on the way out, as did the rest of the team, and on the way back I walked with the band. I met them all, and wrote down their names. And they were Percy Humphrey, Eddie Richardson, Willie Pajeaud, Charles "Sunny" Henry, Joseph "Red" Clark, Ruben Roddy, Arthur Ogle, and Emmanuel Paul. And George E. Lewis on the E-flat clarinet.

Tree did a marvelous job of staging the whole proceeding, and, as we came home, he got an umbrella and joined the dancers out front and showed them how the thing was done. Prancing, strutting, bowing, arching back, shaking his head from side to side, then nodding briskly, he was a half-fast marvel. He was, of course, in his class A uniform, and the spectators along the way loved it, and joined in, and a fine hell of a time was had by all.

My heart was with Coop the whole time, and I knew he was with us. I knew he loved what we were doing, and I knew he'd go to heaven, grin at God, and say, "Hi there. I'm Coop, your light-heavy."

TWENTY-SEVEN

When you got a good friend
That will stay right by your side
Give her all of your spare time
Love and treat her right.

Robert Johnson, "When You Got A Good Friend"

After the procession broke up, I found Cornelia standing under a tree looking forlorn. She had marched with Lainie and me through most of the funeral, but we hadn't had much chance to talk. She greeted me with a wan smile.

"It's all so sad," she said.

"I know," I said. "The music helped a little."

"Not nearly enough."

"Have you got time for some lemonade?"

"No. But I'll make time."

There was a Christian Ladies Exchange (they didn't really exchange ladies) across the street, and a sign said they were serving lemonade. I led Cornelia across to it, and we were seated in the courtyard in the shade, and when I had put a dollar in the contribution can on the table, they gave us a whole pitcher of first-class lemonade.

"So now you'll be going back?"

"Yes," I said. "I don't think there's any rush. But Wash will get us organized pretty quick."

"And I won't see you again."

"Well, unless we get back to New Orleans. Or—"

"I won't be in New Orleans after next month."

"Where will you be?"

"In Rhode Island."

"Oh, with your family."

"Well yes and no. I'm going to the Rhode Island School of Design, in Providence."

"Oh. Is that like a college?"

"It is a college, but you major in art. Design, painting, whatever."

"You don't seem very happy about it."

"Oh, I'm very happy. It's one of the best art schools in the country."

"Then why the long face?"

She smiled. "We're going off in opposite directions."

I studied her face. Was she really telling me she would miss me? I, super-klutz, with a contusion for every occasion? I wasn't being disingenuous. I simply couldn't take it in. "You're saying you'll miss me?"

"Very much."

And she looked at me steadily, and my heart soared. "You're being dead honest? Or just kind?"

"Dead honest."

"Well, I'll be damned."

"I like you very much, Cully. I don't know why you find it so hard to believe."

"Well, for one thing, I own a mirror."

"Are you searching for compliments? You must know you're very good-looking."

I sat there, squinting around the bandage on my nose, and considered the grace of God. He does things like that. He makes love blind. "Cornelia," I said, "I've never been paid a greater compliment in my life."

"Well. Now that you know how I feel, do you think we can make this work? Do you think we can get to see one another again?"

"Hell, yes!" I said, too vigorously. "If I have to by God walk to Providence."

She smiled sweetly. "There are buses and trains. And even military transport airplanes."

"Can you hitchhike on them?"

"I think so. I'll bet my father could help."

I reached over and took her hand—the first time I had been so bold—and said, "I promise I will do it. Whatever it takes."

She squeezed my hand, and said, "I know you will, Cully."

I was transported. The touch of her hand set my whole body to singing. Nothing lascivious: just pure and aching and beautifully foolish love. I could hear little voices in the outback of my head saying "priesthood" and "Villanova," but at that moment I was addressing a whole other set of God's bounties.

We traded addresses—Scott Field for the Rhode Island School of Design—and, although she said she had to get back, we lingered, and talked, and lingered, and talked. And, speaking for myself, fell in love.

And at one point she said, "Please don't fight anymore, Cully. Get off the team, if you can. I know how brave you are, like Cooper was, but you could get hurt bad or killed, and what a waste. It would break my heart."

And she said, "I know you've been thinking of the priesthood, and I wouldn't discourage you, or stand in your way. But I would certainly give it a lot of thought. You're young, and a

couple of years won't make any difference—if you're really meant for it."

And, finally, she said, "I'm not trying to tie you down, Cully, in any way. There must be other girls in your life, and—"

Here I interrupted. "No, damn it! No other girls! I swear it! And if there were, I'd tell them goodbye!"

She laughed, a beguiling tinkle of a laugh, and squeezed my hand again. "Do you read a lot?"

"More than I should. That's what got me on this damned boxing team."

"I'm going to send you a book. A little book. About chivalry and romantic love. It's one of the most beautiful books ever written."

"What's the title?"

"*Morte d' Artur*. You promise to read it?"

"I promise. On my solemn honor."

And then it was getting dark, and she absolutely had to go. I got us a cab and took her back to the seminary. And, at the front door, she said goodbye sweetly, then suddenly leaned over and kissed me on the lips. Then she quickly ducked inside, and left me there, charged like a forty-volt battery.

When I got back to the cab, the driver—who had been positioned to see the whole thing—said, "Is that your sister?"

"No."

He chuckled. "Oh, man. You in big trouble. *Big* trouble."

I told him I didn't know what he meant, and he said I sure did know what he meant, and, of course, I did. When he dropped me at the hotel, he said: "You let a girl like that in your face, you can kiss your ass goodbye!"

I told him I didn't appreciate his language, paid him, and he roared off laughing and shaking his head.

I stood there smiling, because I knew he had it exactly

right. And I thought that mine was the most blessed ass since Balaam's.

I went to bed but couldn't get to sleep, thinking of Cornelia. And of Coop. Inevitably I suppose, the theme became: The Lord giveth and the Lord taketh away. And I was just telling God that if Cornelia was sent to make up for the loss of Coop, he certainly had exquisite taste in human beings—they being two of the finest and most beautiful people I had ever known—but he had a dreadful sense of compensation. Like when, having let Satan kill off Job's family, He gave Job a new family. Job didn't want any damned new family: he wanted his old one!

Yet I wasn't telling God I didn't appreciate Cornelia—I was by God in love!—but that He had got to learn that we humans weren't nearly as adjustable and malleable as He apparently thought we were, and, though He gave me Cornelia as my soul mate for life, yet I would still go to my grave mourning the theft of my dear friend, Coop.

TWENTY-EIGHT

My doorknob keeps on turnin'
must be spooks around my bed
I have a warm, old feelin'
and the hair risin' on my head.

Robert Johnson, "Malted Milk"

Wash was on the telephone the next morning, trying to arrange a few fights for us on the way home. I didn't want any more damn fights, and I told him so, but he said the coffers were close to empty and the rest of the team had agreed to fight our way back. I doubted that, and proceeded to ask the rest of the team. They mostly shrugged and said Wash had asked them if they wanted to eat on the way home and, to a man, they'd said yes. I went back to Wash and confronted him.

"They don't want to fight any more than I do."

"Well, Cully, they *do* want to eat."

"That isn't the same thing."

"Hell it ain't."

"Wash, we'll just make it a forced march. Hell, we can be back at Scott in two days."

"Sure we can. If we had the gas money."

I looked at him. "The funeral cost that much?"

"Two thousand three hundred. And we got rock bottom all the way."

"I didn't know."

"Fact is, I wouldn't worry much about the fightin'. Nobody seems to want us. We got us too big of a reputation."

"But won't the Air Force send some money?"

"They say we already twelve hundred overdrawn."

"Well, what the hell, Wash? They're just going to leave us here?"

"No, they say they'll take care of this hotel bill. Then we supposed to drive down to Keesler, surrender the automobiles, and try to catch military flights home."

"That's outrageous! We're driving back as a team. A team triumphant, I might add!"

"Right, Cully. I'm with you. Maybe we ought to call your friend, the Secretary of the Air Force." Wash smiled, shook his head. Then, "Listen, I got a call in to Hannibal, Missouri. Might solve all our problems."

As I closed the door, I could hear the telephone ringing and Wash answering, and I thought: By God, I *will* call the Secretary of the Air Force. He might be a very nice man.

I was in my room, packing, when there came a timid knock at the door. I opened it to Lainie. She looked tired, a little drawn, but no less beautiful for that.

"I'm sorry to bother you, Cully."

"God no, Lainie. Please come in."

"You said to come by for Coop's stuff."

"Right. I've got it right here."

I dragged Coop's duffel bag out of the closet, and put the boxing kit, a small handbag, on top of it. "All there. I packed it up earlier."

"Oh Lord," she said. "I don't want the Army stuff. Just the boxing things."

"You're sure?"

"Positive."

"Okay." I handed her the kit bag. "Still a little smelly around the edges."

"Yeah," she said, smiling. "Long's it smells like Coop."

"I hope you liked the funeral."

She almost frowned. "I got to talk to you about that. Would you let me buy you lunch?"

"Well, sure," I said. "But I've got a couple of dollars left."

"Never mind that. Come on. I made a reservation."

I got permission from Wash, who was scowling at the earpiece of the telephone at the time, and who looked like he might crawl in there and do some damage. He just waved at me with his left hand, and nodded, and then pointed at the door. And I heard him say, "Why you miserable son-of-a-bitch, I hope your goddamn gym catches fire and burns your balls off!"

Nothing halfway about Wash.

Lainie had called a cab, and we went to a place in the Garden District on St. Charles Street called Delmonico. I took one look at the menu and said, "Oh, Lainie. This is just too damned much."

She smiled. "It's very reasonable, in fact. I'm going to have the blackened catfish. Why don't you join me . . . Catfish?"

I nodded, and the waiter went away, and I said, "Coop told you about that, didn't he."

"Your nickname? Oh, yes. And just about everything else about you. He was your number-one fan."

"And I his. I still can't accept that he's dead. I still feel him all around me."

"So do I. He was full of energy when he died—still in the ring in his mind. He's not just going to fade into the woodwork."

"You believe that?" I said. "You believe in how leftover energy survives death?"

"I certainly do."

"Well, that's brilliant. I mean, the second law of thermodynamics tells us that no energy ever really dies."

She smiled at me. "So does voodoo."

I damned near fell off my chair. "Voodoo?"

"Ask your friend Tremaine."

I was staring. "Tree is a voodoo?"

"Well, he knows voodoo. He's an adept."

"By God, I knew it!" I said, too loudly. Then, toning down as people at the adjoining tables glanced at us. "I mean, I knew he was some kind of an . . . an adept."

She smiled. "He told me what the funeral cost."

"He did?" I took a sip of the delicious white wine she had ordered. "I wish he hadn't done that."

"He didn't want to. I . . . I persuaded him to tell me."

"It came out to a bit more than we—"

"Than you had."

"Oh, no. We paid every penny. It's just that—" I stopped, had another sip of the wine. "Why am I talking about this?"

"Because I wanted you to," she said.

"Oh."

She reached into her purse, took out a white envelope. "I want you, and your team, to have this. Please don't argue about it, please don't even say thank you. It is the least I could do. And I am doing it."

I took the envelope, hefted it. "Is this money?"

"Twenty-three hundred dollars. I wish it were more."

"Good God! You can't do this!"

"I can, and I insist. You need the money to get home. And it means absolutely nothing to me. I make that much on a good day. And, if I'd had a lot of good days lately, which I haven't, there would be twice as much in that envelope." She nodded at me briskly. "Now, that's quite enough of that. Let's enjoy our lunch."

The catfish came, and more wine. I started to speak but she put a forefinger to her lips, then pointed it at me. I was to be silent, and I almost managed it.

"My God," I said. "If I weren't already in love with Cornelia, I'd be in love with you."

"May I tell her that?"

I considered the thing for a moment. Then I said: "Yes. Please do tell her that. Because I haven't got the guts to tell her myself."

She took me home in a cab, and I was somewhat the worse for the wear and the white wine. She saw me up to my room to get Coop's kit, which we had left there. Then, while I stood by the door swaying, she kissed me. The second time in my life, and the second time in two days. But this was nothing like Cornelia's chaste kiss: this was a dedicated, full bore, lubricity of a kiss. And as she broke away, skipped out the door, and wriggled her fingers at me, I stood stunned, thinking that if this was what kissing was all about, your natural man didn't have a goddamned chance.

I never saw Lainie again.

TWENTY-NINE

When the train, it left the station
with two lights on behind
Well, the blue light was my blues
and the red light was my mind
All my love's in vain.

Robert Johnson, "Love In Vain Blues"

I gave the envelope to Wash. He opened it, snorted, counted the money carefully, then looked up at me.

"What the hell have you done now?" he said. "Rob a mom and pop?"

"A beautiful lady just handed it to me."

He squinted at me. "Lainie?"

"The same."

"Damn," he said. "She can't do this."

"You argue with her," I said. "I lost."

Wash smiled, then started shaking his head and chuckling. "I just bet you did."

"I have been drinking, and I am going to take a nap," I said.

"You do that, Cully. I can see you got the wobbles. And you can nap all night. Now that we can pay our bills."

I slept the night like a rock, got up around seven o'clock, took a long shower, got dressed in my very best uniform, and set out to go to mass at St. Louis Cathedral.

I ran into Tree at the elevator.

"Hear we're leavin' at noon."

"Yeah."

"Have you said your goodbyes?"

I looked at him closely. "My goodbyes?"

"I'm going out to Coop's grave. I'd welcome the company."

"Say goodbye for me. I'm going to mass at the cathedral."

He nodded, and we went down together without another word.

It happened to be a high mass, in celebration of something, and I soaked myself in it. The organist and choir were at the top of their form, and even the priest, after a couple of wayward warbles, got on track. I think it was the *Missa de Angelis*, or part of it, and it took me with it wherever it wanted to go. I received communion, walked back and started to enter my pew . . . and damned near fell down. Because there, kneeling upright and not even looking at me, was Cornelia.

I managed to kneel down without breaking anything, told God I appreciated nearly everything, then sat up and looked at her. After a moment, she turned and looked at me. And I was so in love I couldn't speak. I reached a hand toward her, and she took it, and I led her out of the church.

"Good morning," she said, as we got out on the sidewalk.

"Good morning," I said.

"What am I doing here?" she said.

"You're psychic."

"I called the hotel and caught your friend Tree on the way out. He told me where you were."

"Good Tree."

"You weren't going to leave without saying goodbye?"

"God no! You were the first stop."

She smiled. "I know. Tree told me that, too. But I just couldn't wait for you to come by. And why waste three hours?"

"Good thinking."

She suggested we walk down to the French Market, which was only a couple of blocks away, and have chicory coffee and beignets. I couldn't handle the coffee but the beignets were hot and I had four of them.

She watched me eat for a while, then said, "Lainie told me you were brought up on a farm."

"Well, since I was seven. But we really weren't farmers."

"What, then?"

"My mother and father are both lawyers. They moved to the farm in 1936 because my mother was sure a war was coming and that New York City would be bombed."

"Are they still there?"

"Well, my mother is. But they got divorced. Being lawyers, they couldn't agree on anything. My father moved back to New York. He'd been an assistant attorney general for New York state, but he got tired of it and reopened his practice in the city."

"And your mother?"

"She's got a law office in Catskill, New York, but she mostly sells real estate. And fights with the state over who owns the Hudson River, and things like that."

"She sounds fascinating."

"She is. If you like paranoid obsessives."

"What on earth is that?"

"She's a ding-a-ling. A brilliant, mostly harmless ding-a-ling."

Cornelia smiled, then started to giggle. "I think I'd love to meet her some day."

"We'll put it off as long as we can."

"You do think we'll be . . . friends, don't you?"

"Yes. As Wash says, 'God willing and the crick don't rise.' "

"Is your father also brilliant?"

"Yes. Except he wants me to be a lawyer."

"And you don't."

"God no! I'd lose my mind."

"I like your mind," she said. "Please don't lose it."

She came back to the hotel with me, and we found Wash waiting. "Where the hell you been?" Then he saw Cornelia. "I mean, I was worried about you."

"Sorry, Wash. We got talking."

"Listen, I got news." He led us over to a lobby table and we sat down. He heaved a heavy sigh. "Got a call from the colonel. You got orders."

"I do?"

"Yeah. That crypto thing you do?"

"Cryptography."

"Yeah, well there's a big shortage of them. Due to a plane crash in Alaska. Killed about ten of them."

"Oh my God. My classmates?"

"Some of them. Some older ones."

I looked at Cornelia. "I missed that shipment because of the boxing."

"God moves in mysterious ways," Wash said.

"So my orders—"

"Alaska," Wash said. "Aleutians."

"Oh my God," Cornelia said. "My father was there for a couple of months. At Adak. He said it was awful."

"The colonel can't do anything?" I said to Wash.

"No. The crypto takes precedence over everything else. You goin'. And we got to get out on the road and highball."

"I'll go up and pack."

Cornelia rose with me and came up to my room. As soon

as the door was closed we came together and kissed. Very chastely. And we kissed again, rather less chastely. And when we kissed the third time, she started to cry, and sat down on the bed and put her face in her hands.

"Oh Cully," she said. "It's never going to happen, is it?"

"Aw hell, Cornelia. We're young. And it's only a year. And when I come back I'll have my choice of stations." I sat down next to her, put my arm around her. "And a year after that I'll be out, with the G.I. Bill, and I can go to Brown, and we'll be together."

She looked at me through her fingers. "What about Villanova?"

I heaved a sigh. And maybe I lied a little. I really didn't know. But I said, "God went to an awful lot of trouble to bring us together. Keeping me off that Alaska shipment and sending me to New Orleans. To meet you. I have to respect that. And I do."

She took her hands away from her face, regarded me wide-eyed. "Oh Cully. Do you mean it?"

"I mean it. With all my heart." And at the moment I said it, I did mean it.

She let out a little yelp, and kissed me again. Kissed me right flat on my back. And kept it up until she became alarmed and pulled back.

"Oh God, I love you," she said.

At which moment there came a sharp rap at the door. Nobody spoke from without. It was God, of course.

Wash was grinning at me when we got downstairs, and he said, "We ready?"

I set my duffel down (the other guys had divided up Coop's duffel) and said, "I'm not ready to go, but I'm going."

"We got room for the young lady," he said, nodding to Cornelia. "If we might drop you off?"

"I would be delighted," Cornelia said.

She sat between Wash and me, and the touch of her body was like fire. There were moments when I really didn't think I could leave her, and I almost spoke to Wash to that effect. Let me off, Wash, I'm going AWOL.

But I held together, walked her up to the front door of Miss Chamberlin's, and kissed her goodbye. For about five minutes, when Wash gently blew the horn. And when I left her, there were tears standing in her eyes, and the last words she said were incredibly romantic and exactly to the point. "Oh Cully," she said. "We have it. 'Splendour in the grass' and 'glory in the flower.' Let us honor it." And, with a sweep of her lovely eyes, she turned and went inside. I trudged back to the car pushing my feet, holding my tears.

"You goin' to marry that girl?" Wash asked.

"I don't know, Wash."

"Well, if you don't, you're a damn fool."

⌊⌉⌊⌉⌊⌉

Wash had to make a small detour, through New Iberia, having been told that there had been some fire damage to the back of his gym. We got there in the forenoon, inspected the damage, which was minimal, and had lunch in Wash's hometown. He was treated like a king—the word of our triumph over the Marines having traveled fast—and so was Ace. It was clear to me that these two would get together after the Air Force, when Wash was ready to get back in the real fight business.

We were back out in the car when Wash turned to me and said, "You like it around here?"

"It's beautiful, Wash. A little work, and that gym will be first rate."

"Well, I tell you somethin'. You get free of the service and things, you come down here. I put a belt on you inside of three years."

I'd heard it from Coop, but this was the first time I'd heard it from Wash. And, in Coop's memory, there was no way I could keep my big mouth shut. I turned and spoke to the place where Coop used to sit, and I said: "You hear that, Coop? I've just been invited to Hind Tit."

The laughter started in the back, and, after a rueful grin, Wash shook his head and joined in. And Chappie began to strum and sing.

Got no money in the bank,
Got no gas left in my tank,
Jesus, woman, can't you see,
You have had your piece of me.

And there were tears standing in Wash's eyes as he put the Hudson in gear, and we roared off north toward the rest of our lives.

POSTSCRIPT

Norfolk Virginian-Pilot
September 19, 1954

ELLSWORTH–MADDEN NUPTIALS

Miss Cornelia Ann Ellsworth married Mr. Cully Patrick Madden yesterday in an informal afternoon ceremony at Our Lady of Victory Chapel at the United States Naval Base in Norfolk. The bride wore a short blue lace dress with matching pillbox hat, and was given away by her father, Vice Admiral Leonard Ellsworth, U.S.N. Also present were the bride's mother, Mrs. Jesse Ellsworth, who wore a short blue silk dress, and the bride's sister, Miss Nancy Ellsworth, who attended the bride, and wore a rose-colored silk dress. The best man was Mr. Martin Kantor, the groom's college roommate, and Mr. Madden's family was represented by his uncle, Hon. William G. Mulligan of New York City.

Ushers were M/Sgt. C. George Washington, U.S.A.F. (ret.), M/Sgt. Ezekiel Kingdom, U.S.A.F. (ret.), M/Sgt. Laverne Chapman, U.S.A.F., and M/Sgt. Tremaine Webb, U.S.A.F. Ensign Lance Toomey, U.S.N., Ensign William Warren, U.S.N., Ensign John Peters, U.S.N., and Ensign George Mehan, U.S.N. formed the honor guard.

The reception was held at the Breezy Point Commissioned Officers Club. Following the reception, the bride and groom flew to Cape Cod for their honeymoon.

The bride is a graduate of Rhode Island School of Design and is a consultant with Ria Herlinger Textiles in Boston.

The groom is a graduate of Brown University and will attend Harvard Law School this fall.

They will make their home in Cambridge, Massachusetts.